INEVITABLY A DUCHESS

JESSIE CLEVER

SOMEDAY LADY PUBLISHING, LLC.

For Aunt Marilyn

CHAPTER 1

"*B*ut where do babies come from, Lady Jane?"

Jane blinked at Nathan, letting the question settle in the room as Alec happily murmured encouragement to his letter block tower as it teetered precariously on the floor of the nursery. She knelt there, the folds of her evening gown a stark black against the red hues of the carpet that covered this part of the nursery floor. She had removed her gloves and wrap at the door when Hathaway had advised her that his Grace was currently not in residence. It was not uncommon for Richard to be tardy for one of their social engagements, especially if he was sorting through some War Office assignment. So when Hathaway had suggested she wait in the drawing room, she had made her way upstairs to find the children, knowing Nurse would just be preparing them for bed.

What she did not expect to find was Nathan trying every way a seven-year-old mind could come up with to convince his five-year-old brother that to be a human canon ball was a lofty aspiration and one they should begin practicing for immediately. She had caught Alec mid-air as he had made his first attempt at launching himself from one of the small beds in the nursery to the other. He had made it a scant six inches into the air when his head took a precarious turn for the floor. Only Jane's timely arrival prevented injury from occurring. And the only thing that kept them distracted from their pursuit of becoming human cannonballs was when Jane knelt on the floor with them to commence a different kind of game.

What had prompted Nathan's question she could not say as she was fairly certain that procreation had nothing to do with the letter block tower they were currently constructing. But for curiosity's sake, she listened to Nathan attentively and gave as diplomatic a reply as she could muster.

"You must ask your father that one, Nathan. A lady is not at liberty to say."

Nathan blinked at her, his blue eyes bright in the lamps of the nursery. Jane assumed they were his mother's eyes for Richard's were a deep brown. Just as with Alec's brilliant green ones, the boys had inherited much from their respective mothers, and whenever Jane caught sight of those vivid hues in their tiny faces, she felt a twinge of something she could not identify. And even though she knew nothing of Nathan's mother, she had met Alec's mother once long ago, and Emily remained a distant wrinkle in her memory, always there and never quite fading even though she had been dead for more than five years. This coupled with Nathan's precocious question left a dull ache in the center of her where something had been missing for quite some time.

"But Father would never answer such a question. He tells me curiosity can be a dangerous thing."

Jane's mind flitted briefly to what the Duke of Lofton was most likely currently undertaking and thought that statement from him to his sons was a valid one. The boys might find themselves in grave danger if their curiosity regarding their father's affairs ever drove them too far. She didn't know everything that a spy for the War Office did, but she could imagine a few things.

But thoughts of Richard Black's affairs brought her back to the little boy in front of her, who although older than his brother, would never see the responsibilities required of a duke as he would never see the title. The title would pass onto Alec, the aspiring human cannonball, as the legitimate son of Richard Black, the Duke of Lofton.

"Curiosity can be a dangerous thing when applied in the wrong circumstances. But I do think you are smart enough to apply it appropriately, Nathan. What do you say?"

Nathan looked at her, carelessly tossing the letter B from one hand to another.

"But you're a woman. Women always have babies."

At his words, a stabbing pain erupted in Jane's lower abdomen, and the air rushed from her lungs. She felt the cold loss of bodily heat even as the temperature in the room never fluctuated. She stared at the innocent child before her and drew deep breaths, knowing that he could not have possibly known what effect his words had.

"What are you two still doing out of bed?"

The sudden sound of Richard's deep voice had air flowing freely in Jane's lungs once more. She swung her head about, the great plumage of her hat sweeping in an arc with the movement of her head. She saw him, silhouetted in the doorway by the light from the hallway torches, his broad shoulders nearly reaching from one side of the door to the other, the dark fabric of his jacket and breeches accentuating the outline of muscles, and the polished gold of his buckled shoes glinting in the light. But it was his sculpted face that drew her attention, with its distinct cheekbones, sweeping brow and his thick, brown hair clubbed neatly at the nape of his neck. He was quite simply gorgeous, and he always had been from the first moment she had seen him from across a crowded drawing room while she had stood there with her hand tucked safely into the crook of her husband's arm. She had fallen in that moment and every moment since upon first seeing him.

"Nathan said we should be cannonballs," Alec suddenly said, looking up from his careful construction of letter blocks.

"Did he?" Richard said, his hands moving slowly to his hips. "Nathan seems to be full of good ideas tonight."

Nathan beamed, having not yet developed the sixth sense of sarcasm. "I have, Father," he said brightly.

Richard frowned, but Jane could only hide her laugh behind a hand and a muted cough. Richard looked at her, but she only smiled.

"Perhaps it is time for bed," she said, carefully getting to her feet.

Richard grasped her elbow before she could fully stand, helping her as she shook out the folds of her skirt over her petticoats. The fabric was slightly mussed, but any amount of wrinkles was worth a few moments of play with Richard's sons.

"Now then, boys, what time is it?" she asked once she was fully standing.

Alec shot up off the floor, a huge grin spreading from one side of his face to the other.

"Bed time!" he cried and made a running leap for his bed.

Nathan did the same, scrambling to get into bed, but Jane started speaking before the covers were fully pulled up to their chins.

"Little boys should be off to bed."

"With covers thrown over their heads," the boys chimed in response.

"And adventures they'll find within their minds."

"If only they go to bed!" they all finished in unison.

The boys burst into a fit of giggles with the biggest boy standing behind Jane trying hard not to add to the sudden mayhem.

"Good night," Jane said more softly, bending down to kiss each of them in turn. "I love you both. Sweet dreams."

She left the room quietly as she heard Richard approach each of his sons. It was the same thing every night when they put the boys to bed together. Jane would recite the same chorus that her mother had said with her substituting the words little boys for little girls, and then Richard would go to each boy, asking him what part of the day had been the best. They would inevitably answer that it was when Jane came to play, and she thought Richard must have suspected her of bribing them to give that answer.

He came out into the hallway a short moment later, closing the door to the nursery softly behind him. When the door finally clicked shut, he turned to her, and before she could say anything, he swept her into his arms, his lips firmly against hers. Her arms were caught between them, and all she could do was stand in his hold, relishing the familiarity of his kiss. When he finally released her, she looked up at him, a smile coming to her lips.

"There is mud on your shoes, Your Grace. What is it that has made you tardy?"

Richard frowned down at her. "Have I told you recently that you would make a very good spy, my lady?"

"Not recently, no."

He looked at her, and once she would have squirmed under his gaze, but now she stood firmly, watching him watch her.

"Perhaps it is a topic we should review once more."

She stifled a laugh against his shirtfront. "Richard, you know very well I would make a deplorable spy."

Richard shook his head. "I wouldn't say that, Jane. You may come to regret those words one day."

"Nonsense," she said, pulling herself carefully from his arms. "If we do not leave quickly, we may be late for the theater."

She felt the reluctance in Richard's grasp to let her go, but he did finally release her, his eyes searching.

"I suppose I should have Melbourne remove the mud from my shoes," he said, referring to his valet and effectively ending the previous topic of conversation.

"Perhaps," Jane agreed, looking down at the shoes in question. "That is quite a bit of mud. Whatever were you doing at this hour that required such adventure?"

"It did not involve going to bed I'm afraid," he said, and the look in his eye gave Jane every indication as to what he truly referred.

She blushed, unable to help it. A year may have passed since her husband's death, a year since the start of their illicit love affair, but still, Richard could make her feel like an innocent child, unsure of where to place her next step. His hand came up and cupped the side of her face. Instinctively, she turned into it, looking up at him through her lashes.

"You're so beautiful, Jane," he whispered, and the blush grew hotter on her face.

He kissed her once more, softly this time, and it was as if his kiss carried with it all that he could not say, for Jane would not let him. A year may have been a long time for some, but for Jane, she was only beginning to feel the healing powers of passing time. But with the healing also came reminders that other things were moving on as well. Every time she saw the boys she marked a new change, a new development, and a hiccup of guilt would come to her for just a fleeting second. And she wished she could be stronger, she wished she could get stronger before time had passed completely. But whenever she felt brave enough to take three steps forward, something would push her back two. It was a kind of progress, she supposed, but it was a progress that time did not favor kindly.

When Richard finally ended the kiss, he did not release her. His gaze held hers until finally he spoke. "Jane," he said with a distinctive note of hesitation. "About what Nathan said—"

Jane laid a finger to his lips, cutting off any further words. "The careless words of a young child," she said, her voice strong even as her resolve fluttered. "There's nothing to think of it."

Richard's eyes moved over her, but she refused to let him see how truly deep Nathan's words had gone. She stood erect and still, no tremor passed through her. And finally, Richard relented.

He released her completely, moving in front of her down the hallway. She watched him recede into the distance for a moment, just enjoying the sight of him as he moved, all grace and poise, silent footfalls on the carpeted floor. She shook her head and began to move after him, picking up her skirts as she went. She was not nearly as silent as he, her petticoats swooshing as her skirts swished over them. A spy, indeed. Stealth would never be her strong suit with all of the noise she made just by walking in a straight line

"I'll meet you in the foyer, my lady, once I've seen to my shoes."

Jane smiled at Richard's back, watching him descend the stairs before her. He had always insisted on calling her my lady, and she wondered why he did it. At this point in their affair, she did not really care, for the words warmed her regardless of their meaning or intent.

"Very good, Your Grace, but do not tarry. You know I like

to observe the occupants of the other boxes before the opera begins."

"And I wouldn't want you to miss your opportunity to spy," he said over his shoulder with a wicked grin.

"Observation, Your Grace. It is merely observation."

He stopped on the second floor landing to turn to her, his eyes flashing smartly. She couldn't help but return his smile, his playful enthusiasm too much to conquer.

"Call it what you like, my lady, but it is still spying."

* * *

RICHARD HANDED Jane up into the carriage, nodding once to his tiger before stepping up into the conveyance himself. Before he had completely settled on the rear facing bench, Jane was already bringing up the topic he had so carefully tried to avoid speaking of earlier. But Jane was not one to let things go unnoticed, a particularly strong asset for a spy.

"The mud, Your Grace. It is not every day a gentleman of the realm acquires so much mud on his shoes when engaging in a fashionable pursuit."

Richard frowned as the carriage began to bounce its way across London to deliver them to the theater. He could not remember what it was they were going to see, but he suspected it would involve a lot of nonsensical music and drama. He hoped it would only be boring enough to lull him into a bit of a nap.

"Tenacity is another good trait for a spy," he decided to say, but Jane only frowned at him.

"Mud, Richard," she said, her dark eyes even darker in the dim light of the carriage.

Her raven hair was swept up, disappearing under the ridiculously plumed hat she wore. He noticed her widow's garb was slightly less austere of late, the hat of particular note to this fact, but her wardrobe still consisted of unrelenting black, and for whatever reason, this made him pause. Winton had been dead for nearly a year now. He was not exactly knowledgeable as far as the appropriate length of time for a widow to be in mourning, but he was hoping it would soon come to an end. And then he could ask Jane to marry him.

"Dead bodies," he said then without preamble.

He was not concerned that Jane would revolt from such harsh discussion. It was Jane who had first broached the topic of his work with the War Office when she had pointed out a very obvious fact that no one else had bothered to articulate: his rather noticeable absence from his responsibilities in the House of Lords. His loyalty to crown and country unquestioning, it was rather odd that the Duke of Lofton should be so remiss in his duties as a titled gentleman, and it was Jane who had finally pointed out the fact to none other than the culprit himself. She had not even been so polite as to cast her inquiry in a casual question of curiosity. She had simply asked him where he was if he was not attending his governmental charge.

Unable to lie to Jane and not really wanting to either, he had looked at her and simply replied, "I'm a spy for the War Office."

For such a delicate topic, it had all gone over rather unceremoniously, and now Jane simply referred to his work with the Office as his *unmentionable activities*. But despite her given name for them, it did not prevent her from speaking of them often.

"Dead bodies?" she said then, and he saw her dark eyebrows go up.

Richard nodded. "I've been watching a gang of body snatchers," he said, looking out the window at the passing London scenery.

"Ressurectionists," Jane said, and Richard looked quickly at her.

"How do you know that term?"

He saw the moment the blush sprang onto Jane's face, and he regretted the harsh tone of his words, if not the words entirely. He often forgot that Jane still struggled with finding her courage since her husband's death. He did not know entirely what all Jane had endured at the hand of Jonathan Haven, the Earl of Winton, but he knew enough to tread lightly in certain cases. And when it came to intelligence, he should have treaded much more lightly than he had.

"I'm sorry, Jane. How is that you know about ressurectionists?"

Jane's hands tightened in her lap, and he wanted nothing more than to cross to her bench and take her into his arms, but he knew that would only cause her to restrain herself more. So he sat there and watched her hands for any indication of her feelings at that moment.

Jane finally shrugged, her gown rustling against the fabric of the bench. "Ladies talk about things all the time," she said but didn't look at him. "Why wouldn't ressurectionists come up?"

"It's not really a common topic—"

"I've been attending lectures at College. Scientific ones," she said, her words a flurry between them. "Winton never allowed me to attend lectures, and I—"

"I think that's wonderful," Richard said softly when there was a space in her words, hoping to calm her sudden explosion of speech.

She never used Winton's name directly, not in the year since his death, and Richard absorbed the fact that she had just spoken his name like a dying plant absorbs water and sunlight. It was a tiny bit of hope that he clung to, hope that one day she would blossom into the woman he remembered meeting for the first time so many years before. The woman who Jane was when she first married Winton, before the earl had broken her.

The carriage bounced beneath them, and it was several moments before Jane spoke again.

"It was at a lecture on natural medicine. The ladies seated in front of me were gossiping about ressurectionists. I missed the first portion of the conversation and had to fill in the parts that I missed as best I could." Her words had slowed, her breath evening out.

"You filled in the parts quite nicely, my lady," Richard said, his eyes watching her closely.

"But I believed it to be just gossip, Richard. I didn't assume that ressurectionists actually existed, and I certainly never imagined that you would be spying on them," she said.

"Observing," he said, hoping his playful jab would lighten the suddenly oppressive mood.

He watched her shoulders relax, her hands unfastening themselves from one another, and his breath came a little easier.

"Indeed," she said, her voice returning to its normal tone and cadence. "So why is it that you're *observing* some ressurectionists?"

"I'm not entirely sure," he answered, returning his gaze once more to the passing scenery.

There was something about the blurring landscape as it raced past the window that allowed his thoughts a moment of peace to realign in his mind.

"Body snatching is a normal enough practice, especially since the enactment of certain restrictions on the practice of medical schools obtaining corpses for study. But this particular band seems a touch more active than is normal."

"A touch?"

The carriage passed over a rather more uneven portion of

road, and Richard gripped the bench to keep himself from falling off his seat. He looked at Jane to ensure that she was all right and found her holding onto her hat with one hand.

"That's a lovely hat," he said, distracted by her movement. "Tell me, Jane, when is it that propriety will no longer require you to wear such unrelenting black?"

Jane moved her hand from her hat to the bent collar of her bodice. "You do not like this current dark ensemble? I was beginning to grow accustomed to such dark hues, Your Grace. Do you not think it could become my signature style? Perhaps I could start a trend."

Richard smiled at her in the near dark. "It does nothing for your hair," he said.

She raised an eyebrow. "And since when have you become concerned with an acceptable palate for my coloring?"

"Oh, I think you will find fashion has always been one of my strong suits."

Jane looked down at his feet. "It's nice to see the mud has been removed from your shoes," she said flatly, drawing a grin to his face.

"At least my shoes match," he said and watched an irritated blush creep up Jane's face.

"It was only the one time, and you rushed me," she said, rather defensively.

"That was your claim at the time, but I still find your argument to be largely unsupported."

She narrowed her gaze at him, and even in the darkness, he could feel the strength of her stare.

"I believe you changed the subject, Your Grace."

He grinned but decided to leave the conversation where it was. "They snatch a body nearly every night," he said.

"And that is unusual?"

Richard nodded. "Most body snatchers have a concern for discovery and only operate on certain nights during a given period. Although some gangs have come to appreciate the influence of those that may save them from punishment for their consequences, there are still more bands that do not have the fortunate circumstances of having such aid. It is one of those bands that the War Office began to monitor some weeks ago."

"What is it that is suspicious about their activity other than its frequency?"

"They are securing a large sum of money for their wares that is unaccounted for."

Jane adjusted as the carriage made a turn, and Richard gripped his bench tighter.

"This gang of ressurectionists are making a substantial amount of money from digging up dead bodies from grave-yards and selling said dead bodies to medical schools?"

"Yes," Richard said with a nod.

"So what is this group doing with the money?"

Richard smiled. "That is precisely the question the War Office is asking, my lady," Richard said. "Are you sure you have no desire to pursue an intelligence profession?"

Jane rolled her eyes at him. He saw the movement even in the near dark.

"Do not be absurd, Your Grace. Perhaps they are sending the money to help compatriots in France or something."

Richard shook his head. "There is no evidence of international transactions. The money seems to simply disappear."

It was Jane's turn to frown. "Money cannot simply disap-pear, Richard. There must be someone behind it."

He nodded as he looked out of the window. They were approaching the theater, and the carriage slowed to accom-modate the sudden increase in traffic. He looked again at Jane, marking the delicate outline of her pale face in the dark, the whites of her eyes flashing even as their unreadable depths melted away into nothing. His mind raced over their current conversation, and he marveled at what an unlikely topic they had taken up.

He knew very well that it was not any woman who would not only love his sons as much as he did but who could also follow and add to a conversation that involved dead bodies and illegal monetary exchanges. As Richard had plainly seen in his marriage to Emily, some women had heart, and other women had intelligence. It was remarkable to find a woman who had both, and he had found it in Jane. But what that would mean was yet to be seen.

"That is precisely what has attracted the attention of the War Office."

The carriage stopped in front of the theater, and Richard heard the tiger jump from his perch. He moved to open the door, handing Jane down to the waiting servant.

A steady stream of elegantly dressed ladies and fashionably coifed gentleman already moved into the theater, and it was then that Richard realized he had not asked Jane what they were seeing. He gripped Jane's hand in his as they made their way toward the entrance.

"My lady, it appears I have forgotten what it is that we are to see this evening," he said, squeezing Jane's hand in his.

He looked over to her in time to see the small smile on her lips.

"That is because I did not tell you what it was we are seeing," she replied, and he thought for an instant, she was fighting a laugh.

He felt a prickle of awareness run up the back of his neck. He wanted to reach up and swat it away as if it were a physical thing.

"It is not—"

"It is actually," Jane said, turning her face up to him in a broad smile.

He let her hand slip from his in a move of utter defeat. "Again? Isn't there another opera they would care to perform this season?"

Jane smiled radiantly up at him. "You know as well as I that Monsieur Devereaux's portrayal of Tamino is all the rage this season, and it is only fashionable that we should attend another performance."

"We've already attended two," Richard said, trying not at all to hide his exasperation.

Jane only smiled. "Perhaps one day you will better handle your social responsibilities."

"If anyone had told me regular opera attendance would be demanded of a duke, I would have passed on the title long ago," he grumbled, moving to take her hand in his once more as they moved with the stream of people.

"And I would ask that you not fall asleep this time," Jane murmured quietly.

He looked down at her, blinking. "I did not fall asleep—"

"You snored," she whispered. "And it drew the attention of nearly everyone in the theater."

Richard straightened and looked at the ladies and gentlemen moving in front of him. "Well, then perhaps people found me more entertaining than Devereaux's Tamino."

"Perhaps," was all Jane said as they entered the theater.

CHAPTER 2

*J*ane pondered the merits of arranging the titles in one's library by subject rather than by author's last name as a means for more accurately finding the tome for which one searched. She also pondered arranging the titles by author's *first* name as a kind of joke on the unsuspecting visitor. Both subjects were vastly more entertaining than the pockets of gossip occurring about her at Lady Vaxson's tea.

Although Jane needn't have accepted Beatrice's invitation with her period of mourning a ready excuse, something had made Jane come, knowing that sooner or later she would need to reengage with society, and a tea was a harmless enough place to start. Although, Jane was now feeling the need to reassess her expectations of the afternoon.

Lady Vaxson was known for her once a month extravagant teas. It was more of a gossip festival than a sedate tea of polite ladies and their daughters. But that was perhaps why Jane truly accepted Beatrice's invitation. There was something in Richard's constant goading about Jane's natural inclination to spying that had her unexpectedly experimenting in avenues she may not have previously ventured into.

Today's tea for example.

Jane was certainly happy to sit there, cold cup of tea in one hand and equally cold, tiny sandwich congealing in the other, her mind drifting off to other more favorable topics, but instead, she found herself noticing how the titles were arranged in Lord Vaxson's library.

This was another peculiarity to note in Lady Vaxson's teas. She invited so many ladies she was forced to use her husband's library for the event rather than the more proper drawing room. Jane thought it better to simply limit the number of guests invited, but perhaps this was seen as an unacceptable situation to Beatrice.

And the titles were terribly dull in their arrangement of alphabetical by author's last name. Lord Vaxson could at least throw a twist in there by arranging them alphabetically by last name according to year published. That would make it more interesting.

"*Cadavres.*"

As the word made its way into Jane's conscious mind, she did everything in her power not to react. There were certain things expected of a young woman during Jane's rearing years, and one of them was that she learn the French language. Jane had not only learned it, she had mastered it. So when the decidedly French voice made its way from the pair of ladies seated behind her into Jane's range of hearing, she knew exactly of what the women spoke.

Dead bodies.

Jane was already off to the side, and being even farther behind her, the two ladies were quite removed from the main throb of gossip in the room. But Jane could now hear them clearly as their French words were markedly different from the rest of the chatter about hairstyles and dress length.

Before another word could be spoken, Jane shifted one leg, effectively pulling on the tea napkin she had perched on one knee below her now cold cup of tea. The tea napkin pulled free from the tea cup as she had expected and fell graciously to the floor.

Bending to retrieve it, Jane swiveled her head, taking in the two ladies behind her. Neither woman was speaking when Jane caught a glimpse of them, but one was familiar in a way to Jane while the other was a complete stranger. The familiar one had glistening blonde hair, so pale it was almost white, and swept up into intricate folds on top of her head, pinned there tightly with a plume of feathers. Very garish to Jane's taste, but perhaps the woman felt the added accessory was necessary for some fashionable reason. Her features were delicate and unremarkable. It was as if the woman could disappear while simply standing there from her lack of color and notable features. The lack of memorability was what led Jane to recall the woman. She remembered such a woman being introduced to her, on the arm of an earl it seemed.

She made an elaborate and rather unnecessary demonstration of placing her teacup on the side table located slightly behind the cluster of chairs of which she found herself a part. The table placed the dish inconveniently out of her reach, but the motion afforded her another glance at the ladies behind her. It only took this second glance for Jane to finally realize who the woman was who was currently speaking in French undertones about dead bodies.

The Countess of Straughton. Necole something or other. The woman was, in fact, French and married to the Earl of Straughton. Jane could not recall at the moment his given name nor how he had come to be married to a French lady as she strained to hear the rest of the conversation. The only thing Jane could recall about the woman was that she had a rather infamous relationship with cards of the gambling sort. It was not exactly proper for a lady to engage in cards of the nature that Lady Straughton often found herself immersed in, but it was often forgiven, for Straughton was foreign. Many things could be forgiven based on a person's unfortunate circumstance to not be born on English soil. And it was rumored that Lady Straughton did not lose easily. A bit of a snobbish sport, Jane had heard.

"*Dans les cimetières.*"

What was in the cemeteries?

Jane leaned her head back farther as if gazing up at the rows of books that stretched to the ceiling in the tall bookcases lining the walls.

"*Fournir une grande richesse.*"

She nearly fell off of her chair as she strained backward, and at these words, she sat up as if an electric shock passed through her.

Dead bodies in the graveyards provided much wealth?

"Are you all right, Lady Haven?"

Jane turned her head at the source of the question and found Beatrice herself looking her over as if she had suddenly been stricken ill and was beginning to show signs of the ailment.

Jane quickly shook her head. "Oh, I'm quite all right, Beatrice. I am just—" she quickly searched for a suitable word to describe the conversation occurring around her of which she knew nothing, "—enraptured."

She felt her face flush at such an incredibly unsuitable word, but she hoped Beatrice would leave it be.

She did not.

"I'll admit that Lady Weston's choice to reread all of Shakespeare's sonnets is admirable, but I believe enraptured is taking the decision to heights undeserved of such an action."

Jane blinked. "Quite right," she said, quickly, dipping her head down to study her hands, hoping the conversation would move past her.

It did not.

"Do you require more tea then?"

Beatrice stood to offer to pour, but Jane quickly waved her away. "No, I'm quite all right, Lady Vaxson, thank you."

Beatrice scrutinized her with greater energy. "I do believe you are flushed, Jane. Do you require the salts?"

Jane glared at her, unable to restrain herself further.

"I said I was quite all right, Beatrice. I assure you salts are highly uncalled for."

Beatrice retreated into her chair, and Lady Weston quickly picked up the conversation before the moment could become awkward.

Jane let her ears wander back to the conversation behind her, but the voices were noticeably absent. Jane stood, drawing quite a bit more than just a concerned glance from her hostess.

"Lady Haven—"

Jane cut her off. "I just require the retiring room for a moment," she said with a bland smile and a quick wave of her hand.

She scooped up her skirts and made a full circuit of the room before exiting to the hallway, scanning up and down the length of it in a quick motion. But she was too late. Just as her head swung in the direction of the front of the house, she saw the ridiculous plume of feathers disappear out of sight down the staircase leading to the foyer and the door to the outside.

Jane froze, half in the library and half out. Decorum demanded that she return to the library and bid her hostess a good day along with her thanks for the occasion. The fact that her conscious mind had stopped her from moving forward was a sign of her reluctance to take such a step in itself. But there was another part of Jane that propelled her forward, unwilling to let her prey escape her grasp. The thought shocked Jane as it was so unlike her. But, still, she glanced once over her shoulder in the direction of the library before speedily moving in the direction of the stairs.

And it was in that first step that Jane felt something snap within her. Something pure and vibrant, something long hidden and ignored, nearly forgotten.

She would not say that she ran to the stairs in the Vaxson townhouse, but it was very close to a trot, she could not deny. She reached the foyer just as a footman closed the front door. Assuming it was the Countess of Straughton who had most recently passed through it, Jane requested her cloak and hat, pulling both on even as she opened the door herself. She left the stunned servant in her wake and made her way onto the icy streets of London. Winter held the city in its grip, and the ground was hard with a freezing rain. She tucked her hands into her muff and ducked further into the warm folds of her hooded cloak, hoping for added warmth and concealment.

She spotted the Countess of Straughton almost immediately, making her way along the sidewalk along with her companion from the library. Jane quickly made her way down the front stoop of the Vaxson townhouse and began her pursuit.

Her blood rushed through her, providing both warmth and a heady sense of unreality.

She was spying.

Quiet, submissive, Jane Haven, the former Countess of Winton, widowed at such a fragile age from a man that spat at orphans and stepped on kittens was spying, and Jane squared her shoulders, ready to take on anything that might challenge her pursuit.

There had been moments in her marriage when she had thought there was something more to her, something greater, but Winton was there, ready to strike it out of her with physical force. And strike her he had. Whether it was just his hand or perhaps with a belt, he had used his physical dominance as a means of keeping her quiet. When she had failed to carry her third pregnancy to term, she had feared that the beating would end her life. But it hadn't. She had awoken from that beating to find herself quite alive, and it was then that something had clicked inside of her.

She was going to live. Whether she liked it or not, her body was going to carry on with or without her consent.

And if she were going to live, she had to find a way to survive.

She hadn't known then that Winton would drop dead in a mere four months' time, but it had been long enough for Jane to completely slip within herself.

Except for Richard.

Richard had always been kept somewhere safe inside of her from the moment she had first seen him. It may have sounded clichéd, but it was the truth. She could remember the day exactly as it was three years ago. She had been younger then and probably a bit more naive, a firm believer in love at first sight. That was what it had been. But it had grown since then, and now it was such a complex and layered thing that she could no longer grasp to tuck away somewhere safe inside of her. Now it contained a life of its own, and she feared it for what it may become.

She hurried along the street, trying to keep what she thought was a proper distance for pursuing a suspect. Was that what the Countess of Straughton was? A suspect? Jane was not entirely educated on proper spy vocabulary. Perhaps there was a book on the subject that she could find in the libraries of the College. Then again, perhaps not.

She was not sure where she expected Lady Straughton to go. It wasn't as if there was anything of particular note occurring on that rather dismal Tuesday afternoon, but if Jane were to report back to Richard, she needed all of the facts. Whatever those might be.

Her suspect turned the corner, leading away from the park, but as Jane turned the corner herself, she stopped abruptly, ducking behind a lamppost as if it could provide her with shelter. She was slender indeed but not the width of a lamppost. Jane peered around the side of it, hoping her cloak and the dim light of the watery, winter day hid her identity. Lady Straughton was bidding goodbye to her companion. She helped the other woman into a hackney, a most peculiar thing as they had both just come from Lady Vaxson's tea. If either of them required transportation, the Vaxson butler should have been the one to fetch it for them.

Jane stayed where she was as the hackney pulled away. Lady Straughton lifted her hand in a solitary wave before continuing on down the street. Jane was not sure how long it was that they walked, but her mind ached by the time they reached their apparent destination as her feet had merely begun to protest. The cold chapped her cheeks faster than she had expected, but she had kept on her pursuit, unable to let her prey escape. Lady Straughton was up to something, Jane was sure of it. Even if she were no spy by War Office standards, Jane was still quite adept at observing, and when Lady Straughton turned into a coffee house on Oxford Street, Jane stepped in moments behind her.

If it were odd that Lady Straughton should seek out a coffee house after just coming from a social tea, Jane did not think on it. The woman had also engaged in discussion regarding dead bodies in a foreign language at said social tea, so the coffee house seemed rather mundane by comparison. Straughton sat at a table on the fringes of the room, leaving an empty chair across from her. Jane took a set behind the lady, keeping her cloak up despite the sudden warmth in the heated room.

She shook the water droplets from her woolen cloak as steam rose about her person. The room was neither packed nor empty, a steady stream of patrons lingered or came and left as seemed to be the normal occurrence for the establishment. Jane ordered a pot of tea when a young girl approached her even though Jane would rather cut off a toe than drink any more tea that day. But appearances were key just then. If Lady Straughton were to turn about, Jane had to at least look like she were a patron of the coffee house. The young girl quickly returned with a steaming pot wrapped in cloth to keep it warm along with a decanter of milk, which Jane turned away. Just a lump of sugar for her. No need to waste the milk. The young girl curtsied before moving on.

Jane watched Lady Straughton over the rim of her teacup, not bothering to sip. The steam rose into the chapped skin of her face, and she felt her body begin to warm from the core outward. Straughton, too, had a wrapped pot of tea before her, only two cups had been placed on the table instead of just one. Straughton expected company then. Jane waited, and if she held her breath, she did not hold it against herself. It was to be pointed out that this was her first spying expedition. Some leniency was merited.

When the gentleman arrived to occupy the seat across from Lady Straughton, Jane set down her teacup. She needed all of her mental energy to remember every detail of the man. He was rather tall, perhaps over six feet, with stooped shoulders as if he had been bent by physical labor all of his life. Jane nearly upset the teapot on her table as the image of the man digging up old graves floated into her mind. She mustn't jump to conclusions. She was certain that rule could be found in that same book concerning spy vocabulary. The man also carried a walking stick, although he did not appear to use it. His clothes were well made but worn as if he had once been able to afford such finery but no longer. Also of note was the scar above his left eye. It was large enough for Jane to spot it across the room, and it made its way from the farthest edge of his eyebrow, disappearing into the hairline above and to the right. It looked garish even in the dim light of the coffee house. Whatever exchange occurred between the parties, it was brief, as the man left only minutes after he arrived, carrying his walking stick in his right hand. Jane did not miss the envelope he tucked into the inner pocket of his jacket before he left the table and bid Lady Straughton a good evening.

Jane looked out the windows of the coffee house and only noticed then that darkness had fallen. A shudder passed through her, but she brushed it off. Making it to the street before Lady Straughton, Jane hurried down the pavement a few steps, treading carefully into a stoop a few doors down. She waited there until her suspect made her way onto the street and hailed a hackney. The conveyance pulled into the traffic, and Jane emerged from her hiding spot.

Without much more than a passing thought moving through her mind, Jane reentered the coffee house, motioning to the young girl who had brought her tea only moments before. As the girl approached, Jane dug in her reticule, hoping there was currency of some sort left in it or else she would have to bargain with the girl over jewelry of which Jane wore very little.

"Yes, my lady?"

The girl was painfully thin with rambunctious hair that spiked from beneath a stained and wilted kerchief, but her eyes were bright and her smile soft.

"The woman who just left, the one who met the

gentleman earlier, do you by chance know the gentleman's name? The one with the walking stick?"

The young girl looked momentarily confused, but Jane's fingers struck something metallic just then. Pulling her hand free from the reticule, she flashed the silver at the girl, whose look of confusion instantly vanished, eyes widening.

"I've heard her call him Morris," she said, raising a hand to accept the silver.

Jane held the currency a little higher. "Have you heard of what they speak?" she asked.

The girl blinked, obviously thinking back, but her eyes remained blank. "I've never really heard much other than his name and hers. She's got a very lovely accent." The girl smiled at these words, and Jane flicked the silver into her outstretched palm.

"Your assistance is much appreciated," Jane said and left the coffee house.

Adjusting her cloak, Jane stepped up to the street to hail a hackney. When the driver asked her destination, there was only one place for her to go.

"Lofton House, please. It's important, so do hurry," she said.

* * *

"I DO NOT CARE which of you thought of it," Richard said, glowering at both of his sons, fisted hands on hips as he stood in the middle of the nursery. "I only care that you never think to do it again."

"But it would have worked," Nathan grumbled.

Richard looked down at the mess of linens the boys had assembled to make a ladder out of the nursery window.

"Whether or not your experiment would have seen

success is not the point. The point is that such an endeavor is elementally dangerous, and you are not to try it again."

"Jane would have let us try it," Alec whispered then, and Richard looked at him.

"Then perhaps Jane shall not be allowed to play with either of you again."

Nathan shoved Alec. "Now look what you've done."

Richard would have stepped in to defend his younger son, but he knew it wasn't necessary. Alec shoved Nathan back, only harder and with more precision, sending the older boy onto the floor. Only then did Richard step in.

"Enough. Both of you are to go to bed early and think of what you've done."

He did not wait to see if he would be obeyed but turned and left the room, shutting the door carefully behind him. He paused in the hallway to let out a breath and wish once more that Emily had not died in childbirth. But as soon as the wish slipped from his mind, he quickly called it back. For it was not Emily he wished were there at that moment. It was Jane.

And on that thought came another of regret for it was unlikely Jane would ever be there in such moments. Winton's damage had been great, and Jane was unlikely to ever wed again even if he waited until the end of her mourning period to propose. His stomach clenched on the thought, and he moved, hoping exertion would erase the thought from his mind.

It had taken so long for him and Jane to be able to be together and thinking of her never truly belonging to him gave him actual fright. He couldn't bear it, and he did all that he could to pretend it didn't matter. He reached his study on the main floor moments later, settling in before the fire with a rather full glass of whisky and a copy of Thomas Paine's *Rights of Man*, obtained surreptitiously through a source at the War Office. There was concern that the publication was starting something of a radical movement in England, and the Office wanted its agents well versed on the subject should it become necessary to act.

Richard had only read two pages of the drivel before he felt that the single glass of whisky would not be enough. But before he could turn to the third page, the door to his study burst open, the solid wooden structure colliding with the wall behind it with such a tremendous bang, the glass of whisky shot out of his startled hand as he rose to see who the intruder may be. He was already reaching for the poker beside the fireplace to use as a weapon as he turned to see who it was.

Jane stood just inside in the door, her chest heaving with labored breaths, her hands frantically pulling at the ties of her cloak.

"It's Lady Straughton," she said as one of the ties came free in her hand. She flung the garment from her body, the woolen cloak falling forgotten on the floor. She ran to him then, her fists grabbing fistfuls of his shirt.

She was freezing. He felt the cold coming off of her and drew her into his arms, instinctively trying to warm her, but she shook him off.

"You need to listen to me. It's Lady Straughton. She's organized the ressurectionists. I do not know for what purpose or how, but I know it's her."

She shook him with each pronouncement, and his head wobbled on his shoulders. He finally grabbed her by the hands and held her steady.

"What are you going on about, and why are you so cold?"

"I was outside this afternoon for longer than I had expected, but that is not the point right now. You need to follow Lady Straughton."

"Whatever for?" Richard asked, running his hands up and down Jane's shoulders.

The fact that she was not trembling despite the apparent chill that gripped her body did not seem to penetrate his consciousness. He coddled her even as she clearly did not require it.

"Because!" she cried, and she pushed against his chest hard enough to knock him back a step.

Jane's hands dropped to her sides momentarily, and even he stood motionless as they both took in what she had just done. Jane had never been very physical in their relationship. He had always been the one to start something more, and the current physical expression Jane was exhibiting was uncharacteristically vibrant.

Richard dropped his hands to his side and waited for her to continue, his curiosity piqued.

"Lady Straughton is leading the ressurectionists. The ones you have been tailing," Jane said when she finally regained her composure.

But Richard was already shaking his head before she finished.

"Lady Straughton is…well, she's a woman," he said plainly.

Clearly, Jane must have experienced a lapse in good judgement. A lady would never organize and lead a band of body snatchers. Women did not have the acumen or the ability. It quite simply was impossible.

Jane stared at him. He felt the need to swallow but thought it would be too great a sign of weakness.

"I beg your pardon?" Jane finally asked. "She's a what?"

Now he did swallow.

"She's a woman?" he tried to say again, but it came out as an unintended question.

Jane took a step toward him, and he would have taken a step back. But such a move would have ended with him stepping into the flames of the fire at his back, and he did not care to be set aflame just then.

"And why is that an important fact, Your Grace?" Jane said, but her voice was much too quiet for his liking.

He swallowed again.

"Pray you continue with your story, my lady, and I will think of why it's important that Lady Straughton is a woman," he said.

Jane continued to stare with narrowed eyes, but her breath had evened out, and she stood rather calmly before him, her hands loose at her sides. He noticed her dress then, or rather, the unremarkable quality of the black gown.

"You are not dressed for evening excursions, my lady," he said.

He did not know much about ladies' fashions, but he knew enough to notice the fact that Jane quite clearly wore a day gown. It was now nearly eight o'clock, and Jane should have been wearing proper evening attire if she were adventuring about the city at such an hour. The fact that she was not had him stepping forward, thankfully away from the fire behind him, and gripping Jane's hands.

"Perhaps you require a drink for this," he said.

"As long as it's not tea," she replied, and he quirked an eyebrow at her.

She shook her head. "I'll explain along the way. A glass of whisky, please," she said, moving to take up the chair he had just vacated.

"Perhaps a glass of brandy would be better," he said, moving to the cabinet that held the liquor.

"Whisky, Richard. You know if I am going to imbibe, I prefer the strong stuff."

"Right," he said, although he watched her carefully as she took a seat and picked up his discarded copy of *Rights of Man*.

"Are you truly reading this?" she asked.

"War Office issued."

He poured a finger of whisky in a glass and held it out to her.

"More," she said without looking up from her perusal of the text.

He raised an eyebrow that she didn't see and poured more of the spirit into the glass.

"Would you mind if I borrowed this from you when you are finished? It is quite the talk at the College," she said, setting down the text in exchange for the glass he offered her.

He blinked once, but replied, "Of course. Now then, what were you saying about Lady Straughton? And who is Lady Straughton?"

He moved to retrieve his own glass, carelessly forgotten on the floor when he had been startled by her abrupt entrance. He retrieved a fresh glass, filled it, and assumed the seat across from hers.

"The Countess of Straughton. I believe her given name to be Necole. French, of course. Married the earl some time ago, although not long enough to have assured the passage of title yet."

Jane spoke clinically, and Richard thought it likely the only way Jane could speak of such a topic.

"I overheard Lady Straughton speaking to another unknown companion today about dead bodies in cemeteries and something about providing much wealth."

Richard watched Jane, enjoying the way the firelight seemed to add warmth to her even as her dark widow's garb pulled it out of her. The contrast was so startling that Richard lost the trail of conversation for a moment. He blinked and quickly picked it back up.

"Where did you overhear such a thing?"

"Lady Vaxson's tea. The one she holds every month."

"Even in November?"

Jane nodded. "Lady Vaxson will hold tea regardless of whether or not people are in town. Lord Vaxson is so committed to his town life that I doubt he ever visits his country estates. Fashionability be damned. Lady Vaxson makes the most of it."

Jane paused long enough to take a sip from her glass. "But it was at tea this afternoon that I overheard Lady Straughton. I thought the conversation odd considering what we had just discussed regarding your recent assignment from the War Office. I couldn't help but listen, and well, I…"

She trailed off long enough to give Richard a start of concern.

"And what?"

"I followed her."

Richard stood up, a second glass of whisky tumbling to the floor. "You did what?" he said, his voice unchecked as it rose a decibel or two.

Jane stood as well, calming him with an elementary shushing motion. "Oh, it wasn't as grand as all that. I simply left the tea after her and followed her to a coffee house."

Richard felt the blood pound at his temples. Jane had not only followed a possible suspect in his assignment, but she had followed her into a radical coffee house. Jane could have been confronted with all manner of liberal thinkers and revolutionists. He gripped her shoulders as if his physical touch could convey the sense she clearly lacked.

"Do you know what kind of danger you put yourself in?" His voice was low and level, and he knew she understood how serious he was when her eyes lowered, unable to look at him. But she surprised him by quickly recovering.

"Richard, I am not as delicate as you presume me to be. I will not break in a stiff breeze. It will take a good deal more than that, I'm afraid. And really, right now, it is not the point."

His mind wandered back to his recent conversation with his sons, and he wondered for a moment if Jane was treating him like a little boy. He would not have put it past her. But for a moment, he let her words sink in. They contradicted everything he felt about Jane, everything he had seen about her. Her words left him largely unsettled, but at the moment, many of her words were unsettling him.

"Very well. What is the point then?"

"The point is I think you need to watch Lady Straughton." Jane paused and lowered her eyes once more. A trickle of dread licked at the nape of his neck. "And then perhaps you'll find out the identity of the man who met her at the coffee house. At least something other than his name, which may or may not be Morris. The source of that tidbit was rather young, so I'm reserving judgement on her information."

Richard felt a growl in his throat that he would not let be realized even though he very much wanted to see it formulate. "A gentleman called Morris met Lady Straughton at a coffee house. A coffee house where you observed said meeting while doing so unchaperoned?"

Jane blinked. "Really, Richard, I am widow. What need have I for a chaperone? And I didn't say he was a gentleman."

Now Richard growled, and he enjoyed the sensation very much.

"Stop being so childish," she said and pulled herself from his grasp.

"Not a gentleman then?"

Jane shook her head and described to him what sounded like one of those middle class men, perhaps a lineage of wealth but no real wealth themselves. A doctor maybe or a solicitor.

"Tall, you say?" Richard asked.

Jane nodded as she warmed her hands in front of the fire. "Yes, very. Taller than you I would say."

"Did he look dangerous?"

Jane looked at him, her eyes searching. "You look dangerous just now, Your Grace, so I do not feel that an accurate question."

Richard frowned.

"Now you look even more dangerous." She turned to face him fully. "What do you plan to do about this, Richard? There's obviously something afoot with Lady Straughton."

Richard looked down at Jane, watching the light play across the swooping line of her nose and the angular cut of her cheekbones. Her eyes were cast in shadow by the slanting light, but her lips remained full and splendidly red. He bent his head, laying his own lips on them gently, tasting for just the barest of moments before pulling back.

"I plan to do what is always best in this situation," he said, taking ahold of her arm and leading her to the door. "We shall sleep on it."

"We, Your Grace?" Jane asked, her voice rather concerned.

He smiled down at her wickedly. "Indeed," he said.

CHAPTER 3

*J*ane could be very distracting when she was naked.

Richard didn't think she did it on purpose. At least, she wasn't doing it on purpose right then as she lay in his arms, the slightest sheen of sweat covering the delicate curve of her shoulder, the candlelight radiating over her smooth skin and giving an almost ethereal edge to her satiated glow. Right then, he thought she was simply exhausted from the hours of lovemaking, and it was most likely easier for her to simply lie there naked than attempt to cover herself up.

This was a curious thing in their relationship. While Richard felt an almost instinctual need to protect Jane against everything else in the world, when it came to their lovemaking, it seemed like the most natural thing to occur. He had never hesitated from the moment Jane had first come to him. While he had seen how fragile she was then, he had never felt the need to restrain himself.

And now he traced the curve that tantalized him with a

single fingertip, moving it slowly across her skin until she shivered.

"Stop it." He heard her mumble, her face buried in his chest. "I couldn't possibly have pleasure again."

Richard smiled. "You'd best be careful with such challenging statements as that. I believe I already proved you wrong on that point several hours ago."

He felt her stir, moving against him, until her head popped up into his line of sight. Her raven hair was mussed about her head, and her skin was flush with exertion. But her eyes sparkled in the dim light of his bedchamber, and in them, he saw everything.

He saw Jane. He saw the woman, hiding so far deep inside the shell she had erected around her vulnerable body that he doubted she even knew that Jane was still in there. And in seeing her, he remembered she would be gone at dawn, and the Jane that society now knew would return. Only her words from earlier that evening niggled at his conscience. What had she meant when she said she wouldn't break?

No matter what, Richard would still love her. Yet there was nothing he could do to protect her. To save her beyond simply giving her his love. But what if she saved herself?

"If you dare to challenge that statement again, I shall have to seek recourse."

Richard raised an eyebrow. "And what recourse would that be, my lady?"

She smiled wickedly at him, her lashes fluttering, and it was one of those rare moments when Richard saw nothing but a beautiful, naked woman before him. He forgot all else. He forgot Jonathan Haven and the terrible things he had done to her. He forgot all the times she had cried out in her sleep, startled from some nightmare. He forgot all of it, and only saw Jane, this beautiful creature that he loved.

"A lady never tells," she said before she kissed him.

He had meant to leave it at that. He had already pushed her to her limits he was sure. He needed to be gentle with her, caring and concerned. But when she touched him, it set off a spark that soon turned into an inferno inside of him, and he could no longer control himself even if he wished to. He rolled, tucking her beneath him as he devoured her mouth. No matter how many times he kissed her, he never quite got used to her taste. She was elusive and mysterious just as she was familiar and safe. She was thoroughly Jane, and the sensations she fueled in him propelled him forward like a starving man toward a banquet.

Her arms came around his neck, pulling him closer to her as she slipped her tongue into his mouth. A thrill shot through him, white hot and piercing, and he rolled again, pulling her atop him. She straddled him and, without invitation, she came down on top of him, his throbbing erection sliding perfectly inside of her tight, hot sheath. Indescribable sensation rocketed through him, and he held on with all that he had. But then she began to move.

If this was the recourse she had told him she would seek, he would do well to remember that crossing her in the future would lead to unimaginable exhilaration. But for now, he gripped her hips in his hands as she moved against him, sliding away as far as she could before plunging down on top of him. He felt her body moving against him, taking him to her very core before moving away so far he feared she would leave him completely. The physical came nowhere near the emotional until finally he could resist her no more. But it appeared she had nothing left either, and her cadence picked up, driving down on top of him with abandon. When she threw back her head with a guttural scream, her hair flowing down her back in an endless raven wave, he was lost.

The climax hit him hard, and he bucked up, sitting until his arms came around her, pulling her into him as he lost all sense of time and space. When next he opened his eyes, she lay across his chest, while his head remained awkwardly bent against the headboard of the bed. He didn't mind though, and his eyes quietly drifted shut as Jane's steady breathing brushed against his neck.

When next he awoke, the first slivers of dawn were making their way through the window curtains, and the fire had lost its edge from hours before. Jane lay tucked against him, her breathing even and calm as he held her against him. He wasn't sure how long he lay there, listening to her just breathe, but he knew he should wake her. It would not do for all of society to see Lady Haven slinking from Lofton House at the unearthly hour of dawn. He knew she did not care for her reputation, but he most certainly did. And he would not have her branded a harlot.

He woke her with a kiss on her shoulder, soft and gentle, and she stirred just as gently, her lashes fluttering once, twice, before fully opening and seeing him. His heart wrenched every time Jane awoke in his arms. Her unearthly beauty striking him as her innocence undid him.

"Good morning," he whispered, regretting with everything in him the goodbye that was swiftly approaching.

"Good morning," she nearly purred, snuggling into him with greater force. "Is this how all spies unravel mysteries?"

He laughed softly, enjoying the feel of Jane's arms worming their way around him, pulling him closer to her.

"Only the very best," he said.

More moments passed as they held each other, and the light of dawn made its threatening way deeper into the room.

"Jane," he said, but she grumbled before he could finish.

"I know, I know. It's time for me to go."

She looked up at him then, her brown eyes fully open and watching, but watching for what he could not be certain. He only returned her gaze, hoping that in it, he would find the Jane he first saw so many years ago. The Jane that had existed before Jonathan Haven had gotten to her.

And that was when Jane looked away from him, sitting up as her arms moved to cover her breasts, her feet swinging off the bed. She had snatched up her chemise from where it had fallen to the floor before he could say anything.

"Jane," he said getting up, hating that the moment had slipped from him. "I shall drive you home."

"You'll do no such thing," Jane said, quickly slipping into her stays and petticoats. "I'll be fine in the carriage, and I'll slip into my townhouse without anyone noticing but me and Daniel," she finished, referring to her loyal driver, who had been summoned the night before and on many a morning returned his mistress to her home in the muted light of the predawn with nary a word escaping his lips in confession.

Richard stopped, his hands on the fastenings of his trousers. He watched Jane finish arranging her skirts over her petticoats, marveling at the banality of it. She had done the same thing nearly every dawn since her husband died nearly a year before. She may have still been a widow in mourning according to society's standards, but in Jane's mind, he knew she had been free the moment the bastard had taken his last breath. He knew that, deep down. He knew that she thought herself free, and yet, he could still not come to terms with it. He still felt the unending need to protect her.

But Richard was still surprised when she came to him, had come to him that first night. The rain had been coming down in impenetrable sheets. He had been in his study, a single lamp lit, and with the help of the fire, he had been reading. The boys had been tucked into bed hours earlier, and it was just him in the solitude of the house until the banging had erupted at his front door, and Jane had spilled in. She had been soaked and hysterical. Words had poured from her mouth even as tears sprang from her eyes. She had been so wet, Richard couldn't tell right away what was happening until a single sentence clicked into his brain, and he knew.

Jonathan was dead.

Lord Jonathan Haven, the Earl of Winton, had finally had the decency to die leaving behind a brutally scarred widow that had run to Richard when he had thought it impossible. And it was in that moment that he knew Jane could be saved. But while he knew it, every time he saw her, he couldn't remember it. It was as if upon seeing her, all Richard could imagine was the million different ways she could be hurt again, had been hurt and waited for her to be hurt again by something he could not see coming.

"Richard, you're lost in your thoughts again." He heard Jane's voice, but he couldn't look away from the way her hands moved along the buttons of her caraco.

"Jonathan's been gone for a year," he said before he realized it was what he was thinking.

Jane's hands stopped on the buttons, the slightest of trembles passing through her arms. He went to her and drew her against him, his arms folding about her as gently as he could manage.

"I'm sorry, Jane. I don't know why I said that."

Jane was unmoving in his arms, but she said, "Probably because it's true."

He felt her small hands come to rest along his back, but they did not pull him closer. He scolded himself for his careless words and drew back far enough to see her face.

"I'm really sorry, Jane—"

She placed a finger along his lips, stopping his words.

"You can't keep apologizing for me," she whispered, but her eyes spoke loudly of the things she could not.

Of the fear that he knew never really left her. Of the nightmares that always seemed to plague. Of that moment when she first awoke, and the days before were but a blank slate until realization set in. But in that first moment, Richard always watched her. He watched her and waited to see that moment when her breathing would relax, and she would realize she was safe. That moment came quicker these days, but in the first months following Jonathan's death, the moment had gone on exceedingly long. And in its length, Richard discovered fear for the first time. Fear that Jane would always carry the weight of her husband's brutality.

But months had passed, and Richard hoped that time had done what it was supposed to. He drew back, tilting Jane's face up to his.

"Marry me," he said without preamble, without waiting to register the look on Jane's face.

The light of dawn seeping through the curtains warmed her skin to a honey glow, and her waves of raven hair framed her face. He reached his hands up, cupping her cheeks and drawing her face up for a kiss.

"Marry me," he said again when still she did not speak, and again, he felt that unfamiliar pinch of fear. It was coming too much and too often these days, and he worried that one day, it would come and stay. And he knew that day would be when he would admit defeat. Jane would be lost to him.

Jane's hands tentatively gripped his wrists as she drew her face away from his kiss.

"May I think about it?" she said, and he saw in her eyes the slightest of hesitations.

But she was not afraid. He saw no fear in the set of her shoulders, the expression on her features. He felt something inside of him let go, ease out of the strained position it felt itself in. And he dared to hope.

"Of course, you can think on it, Jane," he said, allowing his hands to drop from her face to take her hands in his. "Take as much time as you need."

Although he didn't truly feel those last words, he did feel that he should say them. He didn't want her to feel any sort of pressure from his proposal. He didn't want her to feel she needed to make a decision and upon making a forced decision, to have made a poor one.

This decision would not be about financial security or position for Jane. While her husband had been a terrible man, Jane's father had not been. He had made certain that while Jane came with a dowry, a certain portion could only be accessed by her. She had plenty of funds to support her for the rest of her life if she chose to remain unwed. And Richard enjoyed knowing that. He wanted to make sure Jane came to him for pure reasons. Reasons that did not involve seeking a sense of monetary safety.

He wanted Jane to accept him because she loved him.

The idea sounded ludicrous in an age when arranged marriages thrived on appropriate matches of wealth and security, but such an arrangement left him feeling empty and hollow. No, if Jane were to accept him, when Jane did accept it, it would be out of love.

"Thank you, Richard," she said, a small smile gracing her face, her eyes fluttering down. "I should probably hurry. The light is coming quickly."

With her words, the trance was broken, and they were once more standing half dressed in Richard's bedchamber. Not only did Jane have to hurry to avoid detection, the boys would soon be awake, and he did not want them to find Jane in the house. If Nathan already wanted to know the origins of babies, Richard had no inclination to find out what sort of questions Jane's presence would inspire.

* * *

WHEN JANE DESCENDED the stairs of her townhouse after an appropriate length of time spent bathing and dressing, she was not expecting to find the post already waiting for her at her place at the table in the morning room. There was only a single envelope on the silver server that usually held the post, and the envelope contained nothing but her name and house number on Bridgewater Street. She ignored the letter in favor of the copy of the *Times*, neatly pressed and lying beside the customary pot of tea.

She needed a distraction that morning.

She had expected to engage in espionage on the previous day as much as she had expected Richard to propose marriage to her that morning. Neither event sat well with her this morning even as Richard's lovemaking had provided a temporary reprieve. The news of the day was sure to distract her even as her appetite remained noticeably absent. She sipped at her tea and scanned the headlines on the front page.

The taste of the tea reminded her of Richard's concern over her adventure to the coffee house the previous evening, which did nothing for the distraction she sought. She honestly hadn't thought of any danger when she had followed Lady Straughton. It was still daylight, and they were in a fashionable part of town. She was a well-seasoned widow of advanced age, not in need of a chaperone. But while her mind had gone through the rules of society, she did not know enough to follow the rules a spy must when engaging the enemy. She shook her head as if to scold herself for her negligence, but it was not as if she could do anything of it. She hadn't known then what was required of a spy, and she still didn't know.

She had left Richard that morning knowing nothing of what he planned to do about her observations. It wasn't entirely unlike him to ignore her when she brought him information, whether it be about his sons or a nefarious body snatching ring.

There was something about Richard that niggled at her in the funniest little way. She could never quite pinpoint it though, and his proposal did nothing to help the matter. She loved him unerringly. That wasn't in question. It was perhaps in how he loved her that she questioned him. Richard was always a touch too quick to protect her, and she didn't know how to make him stop. Yes, she had been abused by her husband, and yes, she had suffered. But just as she had woken up after the beating she had earned from her third miscarriage, so, too, did she wake up every morning with the stunning ability to carry on. So why Richard felt the need to protect her so greatly, she couldn't say. Perhaps, he simply didn't know he was doing it. Jane didn't think it was quite that simple though.

She turned the page of the paper hoping to find a more enthralling story to capture her errant thoughts. Page two, however, contained a detailed account of the disturbed graves in Browns Cemetery on the other side of Marlborough. Jane snapped the paper shut and returned to the food set before her.

With only a single occupant of the townhouse, Jane did not require much in the way of a morning meal. There was toast and eggs only for one laid carefully before her place. She sampled some from both, filling her plate enough to look as though she were not ungrateful for Cook's efforts. It wasn't like she was not hungry. She just didn't think she could eat.

Jane had never contemplated marriage after Jonathan. Although, she couldn't say why not. It was just simply that Jonathan had died, and her only thought had been Richard. She could be with Richard once her husband died. And she had been. Quite literally hours after her husband had passed on.

But marriage seemed like this whole other monstrosity that required complex thinking and legal matters. She was, after all, a widow, bringing with her assets ensured only for her use with other assets she would be happy to share with Richard. That is, if she were contemplating marriage to him. But she still hadn't fully contemplated her eggs that morning, and for some reason, she could not move her mind onto the matter of her recent marriage proposal.

Her mind then wandered to the question of how long Richard would wait for her response. She obviously couldn't expect him to wait forever. And it was not as if she planned to sneak out of the back of his house every evening they decided to engage in more than friendly conversation. But her mind had never gone beyond the day-to-day. She just thought it would all resolve itself in the end. But then, she must have been unconsciously thinking of marriage if she thought the affair would find its natural and ultimate end. It was not as if after all these years she would suddenly change her mind about Richard. She loved him. It was all very simple.

She downed a few bites of toast and eggs before gathering the remainder of the newspaper. She poked her head into the hall to find a footman to bring her tea things to the library where she planned to do some reading before the afternoon lectures she planned to attend at College. That was why she was almost to the library when she recalled the letter that had arrived that morning. She retraced her steps, snatching up the letter before once more making her way to the study.

Jane poked about the library when she arrived, wandering over to the fire to warm her hands even though the room was of a perfectly adequate temperature. She set down the newspaper along with the letter on her desk before inspecting the pile of books laid across its surface.

Judging by the piles, it could easily be assumed that she had taken this lecture thing a bit too far. It was as if Jonathan's death had released a floodgate for all things intellectual. If there was one thing the late Earl of Winton abhorred, it was a woman who could think. Jane had never actually tried to meet his lowly standards, but she had also never dared to overstep his unwritten rules by engaging in intellectual endeavors. Now, it seemed, she had reacted rather emotionally to the sudden freedom.

She had attended an entire lecture series of insect sub-species of the Indian sub-continent. When such material would ever be of use to her, she had not an inkling. But it was a rather vibrant lecture series.

Momentarily distracted by the daunting piles of texts, Jane leafed through the remainder of the *Times*. There was nothing of particular note, and as she finished reading on the very last page, she absently picked up the envelope that had been waiting for her that morning. She opened it, pulling from its depths the single sheet of parchment.

Her gaze wandered from the newspaper to the letter in her hand and back to the newspaper once more before her mind finally snapped to alertness. She looked down at the parchment briefly before snatching up the envelope again. There was no seal on the envelope or any other markings except her name and house number in a decidedly feminine scrawl. The same feminine scrawl that articulated the single line of text found on the piece of parchment.

I KNOW IT WAS YOU.

.   .   .

JANE LOOKED AT THE SENTENCE, reading it over again and again without processing what it meant. In moments she was back in the hallway, letter and envelop in hand, searching for any servant who may have been about that morning. She encountered a chambermaid, Lucy, whom she had only recently hired on, but the lass would have to do. She was a touch on the young side with shockingly red hair and full, rosy cheeks.

"Lucy, dear, do you have a moment?" Jane asked and watched as the servant momentarily froze, unused to being approached by her employer.

"Yes, milady," the young woman said, curtsying politely.

"Were you about this morning when this post arrived?" Jane asked, holding up the separate pieces of the letter.

Lucy nodded. "Oh, aye, milady. I mean, yes, milady," Lucy quickly corrected.

"Who brought it?"

Lucy shook her head this time. "It was slipped beneath the door it was, milady. No one delivered it for sure and certain."

Jane's arms fell to her sides with the letter and envelope dangling from her fingertips. "You know nothing of whence this letter came?" she asked, trying one more time to glean any information at all from the lass.

But Lucy only shook her head. "But I could try asking Daniel if you'd like. I hear he was up and about early this morn," Lucy said.

Jane waved away her offer with a distracted hand. "No, that will not be necessary."

Daniel may have been up, but he was most certainly not paying attention to who was sneaking letters beneath the front door whilst trying to also sneak his mistress in through the back door before being caught by politely judging eyes.

"That is all, Lucy. Thank you," Jane said, dismissing the servant as she returned to her library.

She sat down now behind her desk and stared at the letter and envelope. She examined every crevice of the post, refolding and unfolding the piece of parchment, examining the inside and outside of the envelope, placing the letter back into the envelope before extracting it again.

Without waiting to see if it were the proper time for a call, Jane stood and pulled the cord in the corner of the room to summon a footman. One arrived promptly as Jane nearly reached the door of the room.

"Fetch Daniel for me, please. I must visit Lofton House this morning."

RICHARD STUDIED the missive in his hand before tossing it into the fire before him. He watched it burn as a series of emotions moved through his body even as his mind stayed in a single space.

Jane was right.

Not that he had doubted Jane for a moment since she had come through his library doors with the proclamation that the Countess of Straughton was masterminding the ressurectionist gang he was tailing. He had found the proclamation rather abrupt and had questioned the logic of it, but he had never doubted that Jane believed it to be true. He had always known Jane would make a good spy, and it appeared that circumstances needed only to present themselves for Jane to act on it, if not to elementally realize she was doing it.

So it was not the facts of the case that had him reeling. It was the emotions that such a thing welled up within him. Richard had seen Jane mere days after she had taken her first beating from Winton. She had jumped at the slightest noise or raised voice. A touch would fell her to her knees in an uncontrolled faint.

And now she was spying. She may use whatever term she wished, but it still came down to the same action. Jane was engaging in espionage. The act itself did not lend well to the wounded and meek, and as the now burned missive proved, Jane excelled at it, a contradiction between how he saw her and how it appeared she truly existed. The two halves did not meet up in his mind, and he had to shake his head with the incongruent thoughts.

So while his emotions roiled at this new development in Jane's wellbeing that did not seem to match everything else he had come to believe of her, there was still a spy game to attend to.

At the first chance that morning, he had sent an encrypted message to the War Office requesting details on Lady Straughton, so he could better assess the situation in conjunction with Jane's findings from the day before. What had returned was a single sheet of parchment with a single line of text written across it.

Heavy lies the head.

THE MISSIVE HAD BEEN TUCKED into an envelope and sealed with the crest of the War Office, and with that simple correspondence, Richard had his answer.

Lady Straughton was under surveillance already. Richard's inquiry into her affairs had triggered a series of events. The agent observing Lady Straughton would have been notified that another agent was asking questions. Both agents would be summoned to the Office for a rendezvous. The single sheet of parchment that he had just burned was his summons, so Richard quickly exited the library of his townhouse and made his way to the foyer below.

But before he could finish receiving his hat and coat from his butler, Jane came through the door without knocking. She appeared to wish her entrances memorable as she had never before acted with such haste. And similarly in staying with her grand entrances, Jane did not speak but thrust a missive of her own in his direction.

Her lips were firm and her eyes set as she gazed at him over her outstretched hand. She wore a depressing garment of black, but the bonnet surrounding her face was of dove gray hues. He wanted to think her choice of hat color was in direct response to his proposal of marriage, but he sincerely doubted such a thing.

Coming to the conclusion that she was of a sound state if not a sound mind, he took the parchment she extended in his direction. He read it quickly and then read it again. As the words seeped into his conscious mind, a new set of reeling emotions replaced the ones he was just beginning to become accustomed to. Keeping the parchment in one hand, he grabbed Jane's elbow with the other, pulling her away from the still open front door.

"Hathaway, secure the house," he said, speaking to his butler even as he pulled Jane in the direction of the stairs.

She did not speak, and it was a fact he noted well. Jane was smart enough not to try to fill the silence smothering the situation with unnecessary chatter. She was also smart enough to see he was being deadly serious, and this was not a time for idle gossip.

They reached the main floor quicker than he had expected, and he looked back at Jane to see how she was keeping up. Besides a slightly more labored breath, Jane's person seemed to have sustained the dash up the stairs adequately. He brought her into the library, depositing her at the first seating arrangement.

"This will be rather rude of me, but stay," he said and left.

He did not wait to see if she obeyed him, but he had hoped that she would. He took the stairs to the upper floors two at a time, watching as servants passed him in equal haste, presumably carrying out instructions received from Hathaway to secure the house. He reached the nursery but did not stop. Nurse already had the boys prepared for a sudden departure from the room, a single bag of toys and clothes at their feet. Richard bent and scooped Alec into his arms. He would have done the same with Nathan despite his age, but he knew his older son had become more man than boy and would not appreciate the gesture. Nathan was in fact grabbing the packed bag at their feet.

"I'm ready, Father," he said, as he hoisted the over large bag on his shoulder. He wobbled a bit but held firm.

Richard nodded. "Well done, son," he said and then turned to Nurse.

"I'll just be about securing the nursery, Your Grace. Be down momentarily," she said to him even as she picked up her skirts to move about her tasks.

The return trip to the library was slightly slower as Nathan struggled with the bag, but he made it valiantly to the room before collapsing on the rug in front of the fire. Alec squirmed to be let down to join his brother on the floor in what seemed to be a grand adventure.

"Hello, Lady Jane," Alec said as he flew by her in his attempt to reach his brother, completely unaware in his boyish enthusiasm that Jane had suddenly arrived.

"Is it bad then?" Jane said to Richard as she stood, her first words since arriving.

He took her hands in his as he noticed for the first time a deep line of concern forming between her brows.

"I need to go to the War Office. Lady Straughton is already under surveillance, and we may have spooked her. I need more information, and I cannot get that without rendezvousing with the agent tasked with observing Lady Straughton. You will be safe here. The servants have strict orders when I request the house be secured. No one will enter or leave without my permission. But Jane—" He had to stop and swallow at this point. "Will you please take care of my sons?" he finished.

He watched Jane's face, his gut clenching on the request. He knew the topic of children hurt Jane on a level he could not begin to understand, but he also knew that his sons brought Jane a level of joy nothing else had or could. And he hoped that by asking her to protect his sons, she would begin to find a kind of peace with herself, with her inability to be a mother by nature. For Richard already thought of Jane as the mother to his sons, the mother he hoped he could convince her she was, before it was too late.

But instead of pain, Richard saw determination on Jane's face.

"They would have to kill me before getting to those boys, Richard. I swear it."

CHAPTER 4

"*I*'ve never roasted chestnuts before," Nathan said as he scooted closer to the fire.

Jane put a restraining hand on his shoulder before he scooted not only the roaster but himself into the flames.

"I did it quite often with my mother. Although, I believe it's a tad less fashionable now," Jane said, adjusting the chestnuts in the roaster she held for Alec, who sat on her lap trying his best to hide his face from the heat of the flames while still looking brave for his brother.

Richard had been gone for nearly three hours. Jane had been unable to eat or drink when a teacart had arrived nearly an hour before with sandwiches and two pots of tea. She had fed the boys, being diligent in making sure they ate heartily enough to sustain them for an indefinite amount of time filled with Jane trying to distract them from the fact that she had them locked in their father's library.

Richard had been right when he said the house would be secure. She wouldn't have felt safer if she had been at the Queen's House. But even though she felt safe, it did not mean the anxiety relented its grip on her.

She imagined several scenarios of what may have occurred during Richard's short journey to the War Office and what he would find there. Several involved decapitation at the hands of a ruthless assassin while others followed the lines of stunning chase and inevitable capture with a concluding episode of unyielding torture. Jane's imagination could be quite robust when given proper stimulation.

It was hard to believe that only that morning she had received an offer of marriage from the man she loved, and she hadn't had but a moment to think on it. When she had sought distraction from her thoughts that morning, this was not what she had in mind. It was not as if she had planned to receive a threatening note in the morning's post that would demand she return to Lofton House to exist in a state of near military prison. She knew such a description was unfair as she was quite certain military prisoners did not receive fresh pots of tea with chocolate biscuits every hour, but the restrictive nature of their situation was vastly different from how she had planned to spend her afternoon.

But even as this thought drifted into her head, she became aware of the curious conversation occurring between the boy on her lap and the one trying to pitch himself into the fireplace.

"So you see, Alec, Father cannot be killed with a gun because bullets cannot get through his skin armor," Nathan said.

"What on Earth is skin armor?" Jane asked, instead of properly concluding the current conversation and moving the topic away from inappropriate subjects for children, but she really did indeed wish to know what skin armor was.

"It's what Father uses to repel bullets when the enemies shoot at him," Alec said plainly.

Jane bent her head to look at him as he pretended to hold

up the heavy chestnut roaster she was in fact holding up for him. She narrowed her eyes, wondering not for the first time, how much the boys knew and understood about what their father did.

"Do you even know what the word *repel* means?" she asked Alec then.

Alec looked up at her. "Nathan said it means to catch something and throw it back at the person who threw it at you."

Jane nodded.

"Indeed," she said, looking back at Nathan. "And how is it that you know about your Father's skin armor?"

Nathan's jaw dropped open, his eyes growing round.

If the boys were going to create things that kept their father safe in their minds, Jane was not going to be the person to prove them wrong. But Nathan could only shake his head, and Jane nodded in response.

"I see then," she said. "You'll do best not to tell others of his secret, or all the enemies will try to figure out ways to get around it."

Nathan nodded, his eyes still huge with wonder. She felt Alec still looking at her and bent her head once more to see him more clearly.

"You're making that up," he said, just as plainly as he had explained what skin armor is.

Jane tried to look aghast even though she was certain Alec could not know what *aghast* meant. Although, perhaps he did if his use of *repel* meant anything.

"I do beg your pardon, Master Black, but you should never question a lady," she said.

Nathan tried to point an accusing finger at Alec, but he needed both hands to hold up his chestnut roaster and when he tried, he upset the entire enterprise. He got it righted in time without the finger pointing but still managed to shake his head at his brother.

"See, I told you it was true," he settled on saying, but Jane could see it was not as satisfying as a good finger-pointing would have been.

"Gentlemen, I believe it's time to sample the fruits of our labor," Jane said, taking the chestnut roaster from Alec's hands and scooting him to the floor so she could get a better grip on the hot implement.

"Fruit?" Alec whined. "But I thought we were having nuts!"

Nathan sighed his exasperation. "It's just something grownups say, Alec. We *are* having nuts."

Jane took Nathan's chestnut roaster as well and laid them both on the stones of the hearth, shooing at the boys to back up from the hot metal. She carefully unlatched the smaller one that Nathan had been holding and held up the lid for the boys to lean over and see the roasted nuts, their skins popped and slightly charred from roasting, their delicious centers exposed.

"It looks like a turd," Alec said.

Jane moved only her eyes to look down at the smaller boy.

"I agree," Nathan said, and Jane knew he only agreed because his brother was talking about a bodily function, which to all young boys was terribly fascinating.

"And I suppose Nathan taught you what a turd was as well?" Jane asked Alec.

Alec shook his head. "I heard Father say that one day."

"Very well then," Jane said, laying the lid back down on the smaller roaster as she gathered her skirts to stand. "To your seats at the table, gentlemen. Young boys do not eat on floors like heathens."

The boys stood in one hurried motion, nearly knocking

Jane into the fire in their dash to kneel behind the small table in front of the sofa of the closest seating area. The room was rather delicately furnished for a man's quarters, and Jane wondered not for the first time how much influence Emily had had on Richard's home.

This thought brought again the marriage proposal she had not had time to think on. But when she saw the two boys eagerly kneeling at the table, waiting for a roasted chestnut, it did not seem like she had had long enough to think on such a big decision. For marriage to Richard would come with these two lads, children who had been mothered by other women. This drove a twinge through her heart, and she touched her chest as if to stop the physical pain.

She loved the boys dearly, but she had so hoped to be a mother to her own children. It seemed nature and fate and perhaps God himself had decided differently for her. Nathan elbowed Alec to gain more access to the table, but small Alec shoved back, toppling Nathan onto his rear end.

"Enough, you two," Jane said automatically, and the words brought a smile to her face.

She may not have birthed them, but she could mother them.

Jane bent and retrieved Nathan's roaster from the hearth, removing the lid as she did so to leave it on the stones of the fireplace so as to avoid burning anyone accidentally. The boys were rowdy from a day spent inside, and she wanted to avoid danger at all costs. It was enough that they were confined to the library because of what she had done. It would be unfair of her to cause them greater injury.

"Who would like the first chestnut?" Jane asked.

Both Nathan and Alec shot their hands into the air with a cacophony of *me firsts*. But Jane had stopped in her steps to the low table, the chestnut roaster forgotten in her hands.

Above the boys' animated shouts came another noise, and it stopped Jane's heart in her chest.

Someone knocked at the front door.

* * *

"THIS MAY COME as a surprise to you," Richard said as he sat in the chair across from the other agent at the War Office. "But you're a girl."

The girl in question smiled, the movement showing a row of straight white teeth even as her smile rippled the freckles across her nose.

"Indeed, I am, sir. It's kind of you to notice."

Richard looked over at the agent in command, one Lord Crawley, an older and crankier member of the peerage who had taken up duty at the War Office when his old hag of a wife had become unbearable. Rumors had it that the poor man slept on a cot in his office to avoid the woman. In this instance, Crawley was of no help. He continued to insist that the young girl was the agent in charge of watching Lady Straughton. He did not so much as change his tone with each successive question from Richard. It was always the same response in the affirmative. And so Richard was left to have an intelligent conversation with an eight-year-old girl.

"It is not possible for you to be an agent for the War Office," Richard told her, even though she was in fact sitting in the office of an agent in command, who had apparently summoned her. "My oldest son isn't much younger than you."

The girl shrugged. "I don't have another answer, Your Grace. I only have what I have."

Richard looked her over from her clean white smock to the tips of her polished black boots. She was a well-kept lass with a fine upbringing from what he could tell of her manners and the distance between the back of her chair and her ramrod straight spine. But there was something about her that wasn't quite right. When she spoke, it was not with the careless cadence of a child. It was with the banal tone of an over taxed adult. It was as if this eight-year-old child had lived an entire lifetime before even being given the chance to make her adolescence. The entire notion was unsettling, and Richard adjusted in his seat.

"If you are, indeed, the agent observing Lady Straughton, what can you tell me of her actions?"

The young girl blinked. "Would you care to know my name first, Your Grace? I know yours."

Now Richard blinked. He hadn't thought it necessary to know this girl's name, but perhaps he was being rude by not asking. He was finding the entire situation impossible to believe, and the fewer irrelevant questions he needed to ask the more it would please him. But it was only fair to learn the girl's name, he supposed, if she were to provide him with valuable information.

"I do beg your pardon, miss. But what is your name, if I may be so bold as to ask?"

The girl gave another of her odd smiles, teeth perfectly white and perfectly straight, before answering. "It's lady, not miss. Lady Margaret Bethany Ariella Folton," she said, each syllable of each name more pronounced than the one before it.

"Very good," Richard began, but Lady Margaret Bethany Ariella Folton cut him off.

"You may know my parents, the Earl and Countess of Beckenshire."

A cold shiver passed over Richard, sending an uneasy jolt of awareness through his very center.

Beckenshire.

The Earl and Countess of Beckenshire were famous and

not for reasons anyone would wish. They were positioned within Paris before the storming of the Bastille and when the revolution happened, they were used as examples of what the rebel forces were capable of should anyone dare to cross them. They were tortured, repeatedly, until the guillotine had finally ended their misery.

And if the rumors were true, their young daughter was forced to watch.

A rescue mission had ensued that retrieved the young girl from France, but the damage had already been done. And its scars were clearly obvious in the odd mannerisms of Lady Margaret Bethany Ariella Folton.

"I beg your pardon, my lady. I did not realize."

Lady Folton shook her head, and it was the first natural movement Richard had seen her make since entering the office of Lord Crawley.

"No, you did not. It is a common enough misconception, but it would be wise if you did not make it again."

Richard nodded once in agreement.

"Now then, you have cause for concern about the activities of Lady Straughton. Why?" she asked.

"I have reason to believe she is the mastermind behind a ring of ressurectionists, and she is using the monetary gains for her pursuit of nefarious purposes."

Lady Folton made no outward sign that she had heard him. Her back remained straight and her face unmoving. Even the straight line of brown bangs across her forehead did not ripple with the exhalation of breath. She was utterly still until she spoke.

"I could support that observation with my own findings," Lady Folton finally said.

Richard held up a hand.

"If I may, my lady, how is it that you are in a position to observe Lady Straughton?"

Lady Folton refolded her hands in her lap then, the movement brief but startling. Richard found his eyes darting about her person looking for signs of life.

"That is an excellent question, Your Grace. As for my methods, the War Office has placed me in the care of Lord Straughton. Lord Straughton is a distant cousin of my father's, and the relationship was convenient."

Richard's stomach churned at the word *convenient*. Although the relationship may have been convenient, it may not have been wise or ethical to place the orphaned child of spies killed in the line of duty into a position that would allow the War Office to leverage the situation. The entire situation left a bitter taste in his mouth, and he turned abruptly to Lord Crawley, who appeared to be asleep in his chair with his eyes open, his bushy, white eyebrows covering what little was visible of his pupils.

"Lord Crawley, is it common practice for the War Office to carry out such immoral actions?"

"Immoral?" Lady Folton was the one to answer. "What is immoral about it? I asked to be placed in service."

Richard's head swung around to face Lady Folton. He knew his eyes had grown wide with astonishment, but there was no help for it. Her statement sent his mind into a blank. This eight-year-old child had requested to be put into service? But why?

"It is my duty," Lady Folton said, as if she could hear his thoughts. "There are certain things that I must see done."

Richard didn't know what such a cryptic statement meant, but its relevance had no bearing on his current case. And he needed to return to Jane and the boys. He needed to know they were safe.

"I see," he said. "Please continue."

Lady Folton did not stop to acknowledge his statement but instead moved right into explanation. "Lady Straughton is indeed participating in suspect activities, Your Grace. Are you aware of her origins?"

Richard crossed one leg to rest on the opposite knee, leaning back in his chair as if to get ready for a very long and very good story. Only the twitch of his foot belied his anxious state.

"I am aware that she is recently married to Lord Straughton and that she hails from France."

Lady Folton nodded. "Indeed, she does. However, she is spectacularly stupid."

Richard blinked. "I beg your pardon?"

"Lady Straughton is of substandard intelligence. Are you aware of the talk in the coffee houses, Your Grace?"

Richard nodded. "Thomas Paine's *Rights of Man* has been causing quite a stir from what I've heard. What does that have to do with Lady Straughton?"

"Lady Straughton has taken it upon herself to fund a revolution."

Richard sat up, both feet landing squarely on the floor. "She's what?" he asked plainly.

"She's taken it upon herself to fund a revolution, Your Grace," Lady Folton repeated as if Richard were simple-minded. "Your observations have confirmed my suspicions, and I thank you for making such strides in the case."

Richard nodded, although he still wasn't clear on how or where Lady Folton had drawn such conclusions.

"I had had my suspicions based on Lady Straughton's normal routine. She visits the coffee house on Oxford Street on a near daily basis. In the establishment she meets with a certain gentleman always, and frequently, visits with a group of suspicious looking characters."

"Define suspicious looking characters," Richard said.

"They appear to be middle class," Lady Folton said, her voice inflecting just the smallest amount at the end of it.

Richard made a confirming sound while he mentally shook his head at her young naiveté.

"Continue," he said, gesturing she should do so.

"This group of suspicious characters discusses radical literature, including Mr. Paine's text. This sort of discussion has been fine until recently. With talk of war with France imminent, the group has been gathering outsiders to speak to the ensemble."

"Who are the speakers?"

"Some of the organizers of the riots in Edinburgh this summer," she said, and Richard leaned forward on his elbows, feeling the weight of the case shift in an unfriendly direction.

"And Lady Straughton?"

"The silly twit is unnecessarily influenced by all the rhetoric."

"You speak poorly of Lady Straughton, but she is masterminding a ressurectionist ring," Richard noted, but Lady Folton brushed this off as if it were inconsequential.

"She may be adept at organizing such things, but her motivation is inaccurate."

"How do you mean?" Richard asked.

Lady Folton refolded her hands, the gesture somehow implying impatience with Richard's apparent obtuseness.

"Lady Straughton fails to realize that she has married into wealth and property, the very things the radicals despise. However, in some apparent misunderstanding, Lady Straughton has thrown her lot in with them."

Richard waited, but Lady Folton appeared to have finished with that statement.

"So Lady Straughton's efforts are misguided?"

Lady Folton shrugged, the movement uncharacteristically inefficient, perhaps lending itself to her disdain of Lady Straughton.

"Misaligned more like. I believe Lady Straughton feels she is doing what her countrymen would expect of her."

"Bloody French," Richard murmured before he could catch himself.

"Indeed," Lady Folton murmured in kind, and Richard looked up at her in time to see her wink at him.

Richard blinked, thinking he was seeing things and turned to Lord Crawley, who was now snoring lightly. He quickly turned back to Lady Folton, but her smiling, polite facade was once more in place, denying the very existence of any notions of frivolity.

"So Lady Straughton is meeting with radicals at the coffee house on Oxford Street under a misguided assumption that she is making her countrymen proud by fueling revolution in her new country?"

Lady Folton nodded once. "Indeed, Your Grace, and the part that you have provided so nicely is the matter of funding."

"Funding?"

"I check Lord Straughton's ledgers every night, of course," she continued. "But there was no indication that Lady Straughton was requesting more pin money than usual."

"You checked his ledgers?" Richard felt the need to ask.

"Of course," Lady Folton replied. "Standard procedure, is it not?"

Richard nodded in affirmation.

"However, Lady Straughton indicated in her sessions at the coffee house that she would fund such a radical measure as revolution."

"Indicated?" Richard asked. "Are you able to hear her conversations in the coffee house?"

Richard did not think himself a stodgy gentleman, but he did not believe that coffee houses were suitable places for children.

"Yes, of course," Lady Folton said, but she did not elaborate, forcing Richard to ask the obvious.

"How?"

"I play acted as a street urchin in front of the coffee house and begged for a cup of tea. Enough fell for it that I not only had several delectable treats, but I was also able to obtain valuable information."

"Except where the money was coming from."

Lady Folton smiled that eerie, full smile once again without any sign of life reaching her eyes.

"Yes, which you provided nicely as I mentioned before."

Richard nodded, but as he stared at the young girl, he felt a profound sense of loss. Richard stood, adjusting his jacket and picking up his greatcoat from the back of his chair.

"I suppose from here we must convene with the other agents in command to determine the apprehension strategy."

Lady Folton stood as well.

"Yes, it appears we must. A confession must also be secured."

Richard stopped momentarily in his movements, letting this sink in. Lady Folton was right. Although they had evidence against Straughton, there was nothing conclusive. Observation was not evidence until something treasonous was confirmed.

"You said Lady Straughton meets with a gentleman. Who is he?"

Lady Folton did not hesitate.

"His name is Morris, profession unknown. He appears to be a radical as well. Man for hire. Dodgy sort that is best avoided."

Richard wanted to grimace, but he thought the expression would not be well received by someone as unresponsive as Lady Folton and continued to don his greatcoat.

"Well done, Your Grace, on acquiring the information to connect our cases for a firm resolution."

Richard stopped again as he shrugged into his coat, momentarily looking at Lady Folton as she, too, stood, adjusting the smock over her dress.

"It wasn't me that did, actually," he said, finding the words came slowly from his mouth. "It was someone else."

Lady Folton stopped her straightening to look at him quizzically. "Someone else?"

Richard nodded as he finished donning his coat and working the buttons. "It was Lady Jane Haven."

A look passed over Lady Folton's face then that, while it could not be described as lively, it was certainly a degree more robust than her previous expressions. And in it, Richard noticed a touch of appreciation and almost understanding, which puzzled him.

"I see," Lady Folton said. "Has she ever considered signing on for the War Office?"

* * *

JANE PAUSED, her entire body stilling in its space, neither moving the air about it nor absorbing it. She waited, listening for any sound in the house. The knock had come seconds earlier, and a servant should have been at the door by then to accept the caller. But Jane didn't know what Richard had meant when he said the servants knew what to do when he requested the house be secured. Did they simply pretend no one was in residence?

When the need for air became too great, Jane finally drew a breath, the movement somehow breaking the trance she had been in long enough to take in the sight of the boys, kneeling at the table before her. Only now they were still, too, and quiet as the College library. Their eyes had grown wide even as their mouths slimmed to small slits as if they knew, too, that something was wrong.

When no further sound came, Jane returned the chestnut roaster to the hearth, picking up her skirts as if to prevent them from making any noise even though it was not as if the person at the front door could hear her skirts rustling from as deep within the home as the library was.

She carefully stepped behind the boys, pulling them onto the sofa with her as they all sat. And then nothing. Jane heard the sound of her breath as if a parade of carriages were stampeding through the library. She tried to force herself to quiet, but the more she concentrated, the louder her breath became. Alec began to shiver under her arm, and she hugged him tighter.

"It's all right," she whispered, even though she didn't know if that was true or not. "Your father will be home soon."

Nathan curled closer in her other arm, leaning over to whisper to his brother, "There's nothing to worry about, Alec."

Jane smiled at the exchange taking place in her lap even as her heart raced at the silence that engulfed them. Another knock had not sounded nor had there been footsteps anywhere about the house. Jane could not keep her thoughts focused as they raced from one possibility to the next.

Had Lady Straughton come to confront her? It did not seem likely that a lady of the peerage would go about the city terrorizing other women. But what if Lady Straughton had sent that gentleman she had met with at the coffee house? The big bloke with the menacing eyes? Morris.

Jane swallowed.

What would he do? And if Jane had been right about Lady Straughton, the woman would have an entire legion of men to do her bidding. How could Jane be certain who it was that would come for her?

And how much did Lady Straughton suspect to launch such a campaign against Jane? For all Straughton knew, Jane had simply overheard a conversation and followed the woman to a coffee house. Nothing more. Jane was being irrational. There was nothing wrong.

The sound of a gunshot blasting through the house was unmistakable, and Jane jumped, pinching the boys in her arms even as both of them let out twin screams of terror. Alec immediately started whimpering as Nathan plunged right into tears. Jane's heart raced faster now, and she felt a cold sweat trickle down her back, soaking her gown. She stood, leaving the boys on the sofa as she flew to the only doors in the room. They were already locked, but Jane grabbed the chair by the door and wedged it under the door handles as an added measure of defense.

She returned to the sofa and scooped both boys into her arms even though they weighed more than she could possibly carry. It didn't matter then. She needed to have the boys in her arms, and she needed them to move. She crossed the span of the room in full strides, her skirts swishing madly in her rush. She kicked the chair out from behind Richard's enormous oak desk and fell to her knees behind it, effectively pinning the boys underneath the behemoth piece of furniture. She crouched there until Nathan pulled Alec onto his lap and pulled both of them deeper into the space.

"Stay here," Jane said, and at the panicked note in her voice, she swallowed hard.

She could not let the boys know how scared she was. She did not want them to understand fear. She closed her eyes, summoning a courage she had found many years ago, a courage that had come the last time she had not wanted to open her eyes. But now she did, for she must. She needed to open her eyes again and keep moving. But when she opened her eyes, Alec was watching her, his eyes round and wet, his thumb finding a place of safety in his mouth. She looked to Nathan, such a young boy protecting his even younger brother, his face gaunt with terror even as he tried to be brave.

And then something happened.

Jane wasn't sure what it was or even if she could have named it, but her heart suddenly stopped racing. The cold sweat that had drenched her inexplicably dissipated, and her breath evened out into a natural cadence.

"Stay here," Jane said again, and with the soft tone of her voice, she saw Alec and Nathan relax in their hiding spot. "I need to take care of something."

She stood, her gaze falling on the chair she had wedged under the library door handles. She made her way quickly over to the doors, resting her head to the panel of wood. Through the surface, she heard muffled footsteps. Someone was running, and then there was a great crash from deep inside the house. Jane waited, hearing the sounds and calculating in her head for something she yet did not know.

The footsteps grew louder.

Jane stepped away from the door, her fingers skimming over the wood of the chair still wedged there. She looked at the chair, and before the thought had finished forming in her head, she grabbed it. Pulling it away from the doors, she flung it aside and spun about in the room. Her eyes made a quick scan of the library and came to rest on the fireplace. She ran to it.

Kneeling in front of the hearth, she lifted the heavier of the two chestnut roasters, placing the metal roaster directly into the flames. The roaster was adorned with the impression of a ship with full sails, and she watched as the fire

69

consumed it. The metal was thick and solid in her hand as she moved it deeper into the flames.

Jane counted the beats of her heart as she watched the metal warm from the fire, watched as smoke rose from the chestnuts still inside as they heated. Moving swiftly, she pulled the roaster from the flames and made her way back to the doors, listening once more with her ear to the panel.

The footsteps were on the stairs, loud and certain. Jane dropped to her knees, her eye finding the keyhole, a small outlet to the corridor beyond. The stairs opened onto the corridor in front of the library, affording her a brief but useful view of whoever was coming up the stairs. When she thought the footsteps could not grow louder, a head emerged and then a set of impossibly wide shoulders. Jane swallowed as the man from the coffee house came into her line of sight.

Lady Straughton had sent Morris then.

Jane rose quickly, unlocking the doors as softly as she could, and stepped back. She waited just beyond the reach of the doors should someone open them, the chestnut roaster held between both of her hands.

But in that moment, several things happened at once, the first of which was just a dim, conscious thought that someone had come through the front doors in a burst. She recognized the sound the heavy doors made as they bounced off the walls in the foyer. Either reinforcements had come to aid the stranger of the coffee house or Richard had returned. Jane hoped it was the latter. But she didn't have time to think on it for the door handles before her were moving, turning as someone stepped through the now opened doors.

Jane stood just beyond the sight of Morris as he stepped into the room. Taking a step back to gain momentum, Jane swung the heavy chestnut roaster. The hot metal connected with Morris' face, the skin instantly sizzling as the heated brass stuck to the flesh it now burned. The sound would have been upsetting if Jane had been aware of it, and the stench of burning flesh would have made her sick. If Jane had been aware of anything, she would have noticed Richard just then, turning on the landing of the stairs before the open doors. But even as Morris fell to his knees, his hands gripping his burning, seared face, his screams of agony filling the room, Jane held the chestnut roaster high, only one thought on her mind.

"Stay away from my children," she said.

CHAPTER 5

*R*ichard had crested the top of the stairs by the time Jane took her swing. He had seen what she'd done, but more importantly, he had heard what she'd said.

Stay away from my children.

He had heard the words clearly, for no words had ever affected him the way those had. His heart ceased to pump as his legs continued to carry him up the stairs. His eyes remained riveted to the sight of Jane, ruthlessly defending the thing she so obviously cared most about using nothing but a scorching chestnut roaster. Richard came into the library as she finished her swing, heard the sound of hot metal striking delicate flesh, heard the sizzle of it. He saw the look on her face, the expression of fierce protectiveness that hardened her features.

And for the first time, Richard was scared of Jane.

In that moment, the Jane he had thought her to be suddenly disappeared, and in her place, stood the mighty and powerful Athena, ready to attack when attack was warranted. And, by the grip of her hands on the roaster and the fierce look of survival in her eye, Richard feared she thought attack was necessary again.

He grabbed her from behind, wrestling her to the ground. Before he would have been afraid to hurt her. Before he would have been reluctant to act. But then, the Jane who stood there was like none he had ever seen before, and when their bodies hit the library floor, she finally dropped the roaster, so consumed she had been with a motherly power to defend her young that even as the force of his body hit hers, she had not relented. He was on top of her in an instant, pinning her arms to the floor before he finally saw realization dawn in her eyes.

He was dimly aware of Hathaway entering the room, grasping the flailing intruder about the shoulders as he writhed in pain on the library floor beyond them. Jane scrambled from beneath him, and he let her go, half walking and half crawling to his desk. She disappeared around the corner of it on her hands and knees, no sound ever coming from her lips. When he finally stood and made his way around the fixture, he saw the second image of the night that left him without breath.

Jane sat on the floor, his two sons on her lap, their heads pressed to her chest as she rocked them, speaking soothing words that Richard could not hear.

And then Richard knew. Deep within him, an awakening flashed to life, and the two images of Jane that quarreled in his head finally righted themselves. Jane, the battered, scarred wife, fell away, lost in his memories of years long forgotten. In her place came Jane, regal and bold, brave and courageous. Jane wasn't a victim. She was a survivor.

He hadn't known it. And she didn't know it. Or at least, she didn't believe it.

But it had been there all along, and he had been too dim to see what was so obvious. Jane did not suffer. Jane was alive, really and truly alive. She had run to him, made love to him on the very night Jonathan had died. Without hesitation, she had captured the very essence of life with both hands. And when it seemed a new life had emerged, she had embraced that as well, attending lectures at College and teaching his boys horrible, naughty tricks.

Jane kept living, a magnificent triumph unto itself, and he had never bothered to notice, too consumed he had been with playing the hero.

He knelt then, wrapping his arms around the entire bundle that was his sons and the woman he could not live without.

It was many hours later when Richard finally handed a snifter of brandy to Jane. But as her gaze remained fixed on the fire in the hearth, her eyes unmoving, she did not take it from him. Her body was still as she leaned with her elbows on her knees, sitting on the sofa before the fire in his bedchamber, but he knew her mind was anything but still. For his mind, too, galloped with the thoughts of the past hours.

"Jane," he finally said, and she jumped as if he had slapped her.

The thought had him cringing as careless thoughts often did around her, but just as the thought came, the image of Jane with the chestnut roaster in her hands rose before him once more. The image had been surreal as it had happened, but now with the glow of past memories, it vibrated with a beat he was too cynical to call hope. But Jane had been radiant in that moment, wielding the roaster as her only means to protect the very last thing on her conscience.

His sons.

The thought still made him reel, but as his mind continued to skip from one feeling to another, he let it go, wanting for just a moment to be with Jane, to be there in the moment with her and think of nothing more.

Jane finally reached up and took the snifter from him, but she did not sip from it. She rested the glass between her hands as she continued to lean on her elbows. He took the seat next to her, watching the way the light trickled across the dark hair that had come loose and fallen about her face.

She was beautiful then. Utterly unkempt, exhausted, and emotionally drained, he had never seen Jane look more beautiful in all the years he had known her. He reached out and took one of her hands in his, laying their entwined fingers on his knee.

"I couldn't let him hurt them," she whispered.

Richard didn't say anything. Jane had already said the same thing four times to him since they entered his bedchamber and little else. He sat beside her and held her hand, listening to the tick of the clock in the corner and the snapping of the flames. He felt her fingers squeeze his, and he looked at her. She had turned her face to him, and for the first time since his return, he saw a spark of Jane inside her eyes. He smiled slowly and squeezed her hand back.

"I'd do it again, Richard. You should know that," she said, her eyes moving over his face.

"I hope you would." He picked up their joined hands to kiss the back of hers. He settled their hands once more on his knee, and Jane took a sip of the brandy.

"He'll live, won't he?" she asked, settling into the sofa beside him.

Richard nodded. "Unfortunately. However, I cannot entirely hate the man. He was hired to do a job. It's only his choice in profession that I can find distasteful."

"I find it hard to imagine that someone could be hired to hurt another person," Jane said beside him.

Richard shrugged, his shirt rubbing the fabric of the sofa

in a soft, hushing sound. "He was mainly hired to orchestrate the body snatching gang. The job to knock you off was just an added bonus."

Jane turned her head to look at him. "Knock me off?" she repeated. "Is that some sort of spy phrase?"

Richard looked at her and winked. "I'm afraid I cannot answer that, my lady."

Jane returned her gaze to the fire with a small *harrumph.*

"And what of the gunshot I heard?" she asked before taking another sip of the brandy.

"That was Hathaway."

Jane sat up, nearly spilling her brandy, her face suddenly ashen in fear, but he just reached forward and pulled her back against the sofa.

"Hathaway was doing the shooting. It was a two-pronged attack. Morris got through, but Hathaway stopped the others just by opening fire."

Jane settled beside him again, and he heard the rush of her exhale.

"When hiring your help, did you screen them for their firearm capabilities?" she asked.

"Of course," Richard said.

Jane made a quiet noise in comment, so Richard continued. "Morris began talking when he thought we would not fetch the doctor. I've already relayed his confession to the War Office. But although he has told his part of the scheme, we do not yet have a secured confession from Lady Straughton. All we know is that she was engaging in the somewhat dubious act of body snatching. We cannot prove anything more heinous such as treason."

Jane stirred beside him. "Isn't the body snatching enough to condemn her?"

Richard shook his head. "Unfortunately, no. The laws may be in place, but certain public officials enjoy their positions and the flexibility they can offer on such a charge."

"You're saying the public officials can be bribed?"

Richard nodded grimly. "Unfortunately," he said again.

"But what of your meeting with the other agent? The one following her? Did he have anything to offer?"

Richard grimaced. "He turned out to be a she. A girl actually. Not much older than Nathan."

Jane sat up at this. "I beg your pardon?"

"Does the name Beckenshire sound familiar?"

Jane let out a reflexive soft *oh*, her eyes rounding in acknowledgement.

"Their daughter?" Jane asked, her voice no more than a whisper.

Richard nodded. "She asked to be placed in the Straughton home when Lady Straughton's activities raised the suspicions of the War Office."

"How long has she been under surveillance?"

Richard took a sip of his drink.

"As far as I can tell, since the child was returned, rescued from France."

Jane's expression was one of abject loss, but she did not say anything and neither did he. She finally relaxed once more into the sofa, and they both sat there, holding hands in front of the fire, silence cocooning them like a warm blanket.

And in that comfortable silence, Richard recalled his proposal of marriage that morning, a morning that now seemed like an eternity ago. His heart kicked up at the recollection, but his body did not stir. Jane had been through entirely too much that day. A reminder of the proposal she had failed to answer would not be appropriate or fair. Richard forced his body to relax, releasing the idea of the proposal with a deep sense of regret.

"How were the boys?" he asked.

In trying to get Morris' confession off to the Office as quickly as possible, Jane had been the one to take the boys to the nursery and see to their baths.

"Cook sent up her famous raspberry biscuits with their supper. They could not have been happier lads. It was a struggle to get them into bed after such excitement."

"It was brave what you did," Richard said without thinking.

Jane looked sharply at him. "Brave?"

"Brave," he said again. "You could have kept the doors locked and hoped Morris could not get in. It would have been a very practical course of action."

"Practical perhaps, but not very effective."

"Effective?"

"I couldn't just let him try to come in without doing something. Nathan and Alec were in here. It simply had to be done."

Richard nodded slowly. "Beating someone with a hot chestnut roaster was something that needed to be done."

"Yes," Jane said, a smirk hesitantly coming to her lips. "A suitable offensive tactic was in order."

Richard raised an eyebrow at her strategist's speak. Jane just raised one in return.

"How is that for spy language?"

"Fair," Richard said, but he followed it with a smile.

Jane laughed softly, leaning forward to set her snifter on the table before the sofa. When she leaned back, she nestled into his side, forcing one of his arms over and around her shoulders. Her head came to rest at the top of his chest.

"We should go to bed," Richard said, even as Jane seemed to deflate against him.

"Just a few minutes more," she said, her voice soft and drowsy.

Richard tightened his arm about her, accommodating her

request even as sense dictated he should not. The clock ticked on for several minutes while they sat in silence, holding onto each other as the night moved past them. Richard felt his eyes drifting shut, and he forced them open. The warm fire and brandy were not helping his already drained body to stay awake, and he nudged Jane's shoulder.

"Are you awake?"

"No," came the soft answer from somewhere in the vicinity of his chest.

"Then let's be off to bed."

"I supposed you're right," Jane finally said, her voice slightly stronger as she moved away from him. "The boys will be up early, no doubt, and they'll be wanting to hear the stories of their unstoppable father."

Richard watched her rise, unable to move at her confusing words.

"Unstoppable?"

Jane nodded. "They believe your skin has the miraculous ability to stop bullets."

Richard raised an eyebrow. "Truly?"

"Yes," Jane said, a soft smile tugging at her lips.

He saw the weariness in her eyes, and he stood, drawing her near to him. They stood for a moment before the fire. He in only trousers and shirtsleeves, and she, her hair mussed about her shoulders, her dress wrinkled and dirty. They would have made quite the sight, but standing there with her in his arms, Richard could not have cared about such things.

He kissed her gently. "Let's go to bed, Jane."

She smiled at him and said, "Let's."

He wanted to make love to her. He wanted to show her with actions what words were incapable of conveying. But his body would not do what his mind asked of it. His body was already shutting down before he reached the bed. He carelessly discarded his trousers and shirt, watching as Jane struggled with the buttons of her gown. Completely naked now, he made his way across the room as if helping Jane with her buttons was something he did every night. The gesture was a punch to his stomach, and he held his breath to stop the pain. If only Jane would say yes to his proposal. If only she would marry him.

He undid the buttons of her gown quickly, slipping the garment from her shoulders. The rest of her garments came off quickly, and soon, she was just as naked as he was. He helped her into the high bed, pulling back the coverlet as she fell into the soft folds of the mattress. He followed her and went to pull her into his arms when she suddenly sat up, pulling at her hair.

"I don't want to cause you to lose an eye if one of my hair pins wanders," she said without looking at him.

He watched her, the firelight cascading over the gentle curves of her body like the touch of a lover. The scene was hypnotic, and he could not look away. She gently removed the hair pins, her arms moving with a fluidity that could not have come from a human body.

Richard lay against the plush pillows of the bed, his heart pounding in his chest as he watched her long raven hair fall down her back in a waterfall. The sight had him up on his knees, suddenly no longer tired in the least. He came up behind her, his hands traveling from her back, through her long locks to cup her breasts. She gasped at his touch, as he kneaded the thick, heavy orbs, and then she moaned, leaning back into him, bringing her body against his. Tendrils of her hair fell over her shoulders and covered his hands. The sight was so sensual he felt his body react physically, his erection growing and throbbing as the sight of Jane aroused him like nothing else could.

"Richard," she moaned, and he let one hand drift lower, moving through the patch of tight curls at her very core.

But he did not touch her.

He stroked her thighs, first one and then the other, his fingers always moving. Next came the soft folds of her opening, and with but a single finger against her, she jerked in his arms, his name coming out as a plea. The single word was enough to have him slip a finger inside of her. The tight muscles of her sheath spasmed against that finger, and the surprise at finding her already wet had his erection throbbing harder.

He shifted against her, allowing his pulsating manhood to rest in the curve of her spine just above the crest of her buttocks. Her soft curves pushed against him, and he slipped across her velvety skin. It was his turn to moan as he struggled to maintain control. But Jane had begun to move, her hips pushing his finger deeper inside of her. He withdrew the finger and quickly replaced it with two, plunging into her with a come here motion. She screamed, the sound ragged, filled with a basic desire he had never before heard her make.

It was enough to force him ahead. He pushed on her back, bending her over until she was on her hands and knees. He pulled his fingers free of her, keeping one finger, slick with her own juice, rubbing soft circles around her sensitive nub. And then he was inside of her, her body pulsing around him. The heat, the tightness, the movement were all too much, and he knew he wouldn't last long. He moved inside of her, but she moved against him, her hips ratcheting, pushing his penis so deep.

"Jane," he said, unable to say more.

But suddenly, she reached back, pulling his hips toward her, pushing him farther inside of her.

"Come with me," he heard her say just as everything exploded.

* * *

JANE CAME AWAKE SLOWLY, aware of several things at once.

She was naked, she was not alone, and it was much later than it should have been.

She sat up, pushing Richard's arm off of her. She heard him grumble in his sleep before he, too, opened his eyes. It wasn't long before he sat up as well.

"What time is it?" he said, his voice rough with sleep.

"It's late," Jane said, staring about the room, at their piles of discarded clothing, the rumpled linens streaming from the bed, and worse, the roaring fire. "It's *too* late. Someone's already been here to build the fire back up."

Richard scrubbed his hands over his face before looking in the direction of the fireplace. Jane turned to watch his reaction, but when he simply shrugged, she felt a twitch of concern.

"Is that all?" she asked.

He stifled a yawn before pushing back the bedclothes and rising. "So the servants know you spent the entire night. It's not as if they haven't had enough clues about it. It has been nearly a year of me sneaking you through the kitchen and out the back at ungodly hours of the morning."

Richard padded over to where a silk dressing gown had been placed on one of the chairs in front of the fire. The morning light seeping through the curtains highlighted the muscles of his back as he moved, accentuating the lean lines of his torso where it tapered to his hips. Jane was momentarily mesmerized by the movement, her thoughts scattering as she enjoyed watching Richard move about the room naked. He donned the dressing gown far too quickly and turned to face the room.

"Oh, they've left tea, too." He said this with such boyish enthusiasm that Jane laughed.

Richard smiled at her, his hair mussed from sleep sticking out from the sides of his head. He looked so young then that for a breath Jane forgot entirely about the proceedings of the previous day. She forgot all about Lady Straughton and Morris and body snatchers and treason. All of it went away when there was just Richard to look at.

"Are you truly not concerned that the servants know that I spent the entire night? Or that I may not be able to leave this morning without it being observed?"

Richard looked at her, his hands on the belt of his robe as he finished tying it off. "No, I truly am not concerned," he finally said. "Jane—" He paused, taking a step forward as if to help his thoughts along. "I underestimated you, and it was unfair of me. I hope you can forgive me."

Jane blinked, feeling all sense of the world about her slink away.

"I beg your pardon?" she asked, but she wasn't really sure Richard could clarify enough for her to understand of what he spoke.

Richard looked down at his feet before making his way over to her, coming to sit beside her on the bed. His thigh touched hers through the sheets, and she welcomed the heat of his body. But she wouldn't let him distract her.

"What are you going on about, Richard?" She prompted him along in his clarification.

He gathered her hands in his before looking up at her, his eyes focused on hers so intently, she felt that words would be extraneous in that moment.

"Jane," he said, "I saw you after Winton beat you. I saw what you looked like. The bruises, the cuts, and I remember how you would tell people you had fallen. Your excuses came so quickly at the end, that I don't think even you believed them any longer. Everyone knew what Winton was doing to you, and no one understood how you survived it. Only I—"

His voice broke, and Jane reflexively tightened her hold on his fingers, following the movement of his face as he struggled with his words. He closed his eyes for a moment, and Jane waited. Richard had never spoken to her like this. He had never even mentioned what she had gone through in her marriage to Winton in the many years they had known each other.

"I didn't believe you were strong enough to survive it," he finally said, and when he opened his eyes, she found they were wet with tears.

Words failed her. She knew she should have said something, but her mind was an utter blankness she could not fill.

"Richard," was all that she could manage.

"I was wrong, Jane," Richard continued. "You were strong enough to survive Winton, and you are strong enough to survive even more, and I am so sorry that I doubted you."

"I never knew you doubted me, Richard," she said, pulling one of her hands free to cup the side of his face. "You were always there for me when I needed you. You and your outrageous sons." She smiled then, softly, afraid and unsure of what to say next. "I have always had your support when it mattered most. Don't ever doubt that, Richard."

The corners of his mouth tugged with a reluctant smile, and she leaned forward to kiss him softly. When she pulled back, his eyes had cleared, and he looked more like the Richard she had fallen in love with, the Richard she wanted to spend the rest of her life with.

This thought had her swallowing hard. Had she made that decision already? The slight hesitation she had felt at Richard's overprotectiveness had vanished at his words. But had she decided to not only be a wife, but to be a mother to children that were not born of her flesh? She hadn't been aware of it, but suddenly, calling the boys her own seemed to fit. Seemed to be inevitable.

"What is it?" Richard whispered.

"I am in great need of a chamber pot," she said, rather than of speaking of the things on her mind.

Richard jumped off the bed, the movement so startling she laughed.

"A chamber pot it is, my lady," Richard said, flourishing his arm in the direction of his dressing room. "Off with you then."

Jane scooted to the edge of the bed, bending over to retrieve an article of clothing from the floor. It happened to be Richard's shirt and was likely too large for her person, but she drew it over her head anyway, running her fingers up the buttons in the front. She looked up to find Richard raising one of his eyebrows at her.

"It's cold," she said, her nose scrunching up at his obvious lack of understanding.

He tilted his head back and barked a laugh of utter delight. The image was so fulfilling after the events of the day before that she laughed as well. But then nature's urges were too strong, and she finished getting up from the bed, all but dashing into the dressing room. She went to the back of the room where a chamber pot was usually stowed only to find two rather startling things. The first of which was a bourdaloue and the second, one of her gowns, freshly pressed and hung among Richard's wardrobe. The fact that one of her gowns should have materialized in Richard's dressing room seemingly overnight was odd but not unexpected. Richard must have told a servant on the previous night to have the garment fetched, realizing Jane may not make it home.

But the bourdaloue was an entirely different matter of a rather delicately intimate nature. She snatched up the porcelain vessel and returned to the main bedchamber.

"Have you taken to entertaining ladies in your

bedchamber at an incredible frequency?" Jane said when she reached the room.

Richard looked up from where he was pouring tea in front of the fire. His brow wrinkled as if in thought. "Not that I can recall. Unless you are thinking of making more regular visits," he said as if it were an after thought.

Jane held up the bourdaloue. "Then what is this doing in your dressing room?"

Richard did not hesitate. "Waiting for you to make use of it."

Jane's hand faltered slightly at his words, and the bourdaloue wobbled in her grip. "You acquired this for me?"

Richard nodded, finishing with one tea cup before starting to fill another. "I had heard that chamber pots could be awkward for ladies, and I didn't want you to be inconvenienced." He finished filling the second cup and returned his gaze more directly to her. "I thought you had dire need of such facilities. Why are you standing there having this conversation with me?"

The hand holding the bourdaloue dropped completely, returning to its place at her side.

"That is the nicest thing that anyone has ever done for me," Jane said and was surprised to find her voice came out as a whisper.

Richard only looked at her. "Getting you a pot to relieve yourself in is the nicest thing anyone has done for you?" he asked, one eyebrow raised.

Jane only nodded at first but finally managed a soft, "Yes."

"Then it would appear I have low expectations to meet," Richard said and then pointed to the dressing room door. "Now go. I'll impress you further upon your return by offering you a cup of tea."

Richard sat on the sofa facing the fire, pulling the tea tray closer as he finished preparing their cups. Jane went back into the dressing room, happily using the much more convenient bourdaloue before partaking of the water left in the pitcher on Richard's dressing table. She washed her hands and face, the water refreshing her from the sleep that had seemed to consume her. She found Richard relaxing on the sofa, a cup of tea in hand. She snatched up her own cup before joining him.

"You do realize we have about thirty seconds before the boys are up, and we will have some explaining to do?" she said, tucking her feet under her as she sat on the sofa.

Richard nodded over his steaming cup of tea. "Indeed. And what is it that we're going to explain?"

"We're going to explain why it is that I am a guest at breakfast."

"You like eggs," Richard said. "Your presence has been explained."

Jane smiled into her tea as she took a sip. "Richard," she said when she finished swallowing.

"Ah, the serious part of the day has already commenced," Richard said, throwing her a sarcastic glance.

She frowned at him. "I need to ask of you a favor," she said.

Richard returned his cup to the tea tray. "Anything, my lady," he said, turning so he faced her fully.

"I need you to take me to the War Office," she said.

"What for?" was Richard's near instant reply.

"I would like to join the Office as an agent." The words felt awkward in her mouth even as her resolve tightened.

This was something she needed to do. It was something that must be done. She had known the moment that she had decided to descend the steps to follow Lady Straughton from Lady Vaxson's tea that this was the inevitable course for her to follow. She had felt it in the same way she had felt the primal need to protect Alec and Nathan from Morris the previous day. It was like every time she would open her eyes after one of Winton's beatings, she knew she had to go on. And just as Richard had said. She *was* a survivor, and as such, she had a bravery and courage that not everyone possessed. It was time she started putting that to good use.

"Jane, I know I may have suggested that you consider this profession, but I never meant—"

"You were right, Richard," she cut him off. "You were right."

She didn't say anything more, but she knew he understood her words. She saw it in the way his face softened, the corners of his eyes relaxing into the familiar wrinkles she loved to trace with her fingertips.

"I hate being right," he finally said. "We shall go to the War Office, my lady, to make you a spy."

Jane smiled, a brilliant smile that almost hurt her face, a smile unlike any she had felt in years. Richard's eyes widened as he, too, likely realized the same thing. Jane was returning to a life interrupted.

"Is this what it takes to make you happy? Espionage?" he asked.

She nodded, but said, "Espionage and eggs."

Richard smiled now, his grin almost as big as hers. "And I suppose your reasons for this sudden decision include a plan to secure a confession from Lady Straughton?"

Jane blinked, her sense of euphoria quickly replaced with one of confusion. "How do you know that?"

Richard still grinned. "I know you, Jane, whether you like it or not. And the boys tell me things."

Her face reddened. She felt the burn as the blush crept up her cheeks. "Tell you what?"

Now Richard smiled at her devilishly, his eyes sparkling with mischief. "Oh, they tell me plenty. That is how I know becoming a spy to accomplish something you see being possible is not an obstacle you would give worthy credit to."

Jane frowned. "I swore those boys to secrecy."

"They're boys, and they think you're quite the thing. Of course, they're going to tell."

She scrunched her mouth into a pout. "That's the last time I let them try to fly by jumping off the roof."

Richard's face fell, his eyes growing wide with concern. Jane was quick to smile in reassurance.

"Just sporting you, Your Grace."

She stood up with a flourish of shirttails.

"I'd like a bath if possible," she said over her shoulder as she made her way to the pile of her discarded clothes. She picked up the underthings and held them to her nose. They would just have to do as she had not seen any clean ones with her gown.

"A bath is certainly possible," Richard said as he, too, rose and made his way to the bell pull in the corner. "I'm sure the boys will have awakened Nurse by now. I'll get dressed and see to them. Will you come down for breakfast then?"

Jane finished investigating her petticoats and turned to him. "Of course. I like eggs, remember?"

His eyes sparkled again. "It's not as if you let me forget it," he said, but then his face turned serious. "Jane, do you indeed have a plan for getting a confession from Lady Straughton?"

Jane set her underthings on the chair by the dressing room and turned, putting her hands on her hips.

"I do, Your Grace, but I'm not sure you would understand it entirely. It involves a rather improper practice."

"Improper?"

"Yes," she took a step closer to him, "How do you feel about ladies gambling at cards?"

CHAPTER 6

"*I* cannot believe I am letting you do this," Richard grumbled, peering out the window of the carriage at the largely dull house on Piccadilly.

"*I* cannot believe you are allowing me to do this, but as you are, I should be on my way."

Jane moved to exit the carriage, but Richard placed his hand on her arm.

"Are you certain about this?" he asked, and Jane studied his face in the dim light of the carriage.

She had been an agent for the War Office of the British Empire for all of six hours, thirty two minutes, and several seconds, and Richard had been questioning her resolve for six hours thirty one minutes and several seconds. It was becoming wearisome.

"I assure you, Your Grace, that I am more than ready for this."

When her words had no visible effect on him, Jane reached up and, with her gloved hand, cupped the side of his face. The touch had him softening noticeably.

"What were you just saying about my courage, Richard?"

This drew out a smile, and she let her hand fall away from his face. She smiled in return and went over their plan again, as if speaking of the facts would settle his nerves.

"I am to engage Lady Straughton in a game of Pharo, and I am to pressure her through the game into confessing."

Richard raised an eyebrow.

"Do you really believe me so inept at cards that I will not be able to do this?" she responded to his expression.

Richard shrugged. "I've never seen you even show interest in cards before today, and I really have no way to judge the success of this endeavor."

Jane raised an eyebrow back at him. "There appears to be several things you were not aware of before today, Your Grace. You should be taking notes perhaps."

Richard frowned but said, "The room will be filled with agents. The banker at the table will also be an agent, so if you do get Lady Straughton—"

"When I get Lady Straughton," Jane corrected.

Richard nodded in acknowledgment.

"When you get Lady Straughton to confess, there will be more than one agent within hearing to observe the confession. Is that clear?"

Jane nodded, looking out the window once more at the house on Piccadilly. Richard followed her gaze and said, "And how is it that no one in the Office knew about this establishment?"

Jane turned her head swiftly toward him. "Why on Earth would Viscount Fitzsimmons proclaim the existence of his little gambling establishment to members of a government body? What Fitzsimmons is doing here is not exactly legal. He has opened a portion of his home as a gambling establishment for genteel ladies. Such an action is not entirely on the up and up, Your Grace. I would *hope* you knew nothing of this."

"And you are certain that Lady Straughton makes frequent visits?"

Jane nodded.

"It is one of the few things I do know about her. She's rather legendary at Pharo."

"Lady Folton was unable to confirm your suspicions," Richard said, referring to their meeting earlier that day with the young girl.

Jane frowned, unable to stop the sudden feeling of sadness at the mention of the child.

"I should hope not. It's an unsavory topic for children to be aware of," she said.

Richard continued to look out the window, and Jane noticed the way the moonlight slid off the angles of his face. He looked even more handsome in that moment, and she felt her heart hurt with the joy of it, her feelings a sliding spectrum of emotion.

"But I will not be able to do anything if you do not let me out," she said then, pushing away all the other feelings that threatened to overwhelm her.

Six hours ago she had taken an oath. An oath she meant to uphold, and thoughts of the man she loved would not help her in this endeavor. She needed to be clear-headed and objective. She needed to do this. And not just for Richard or for country or the monarch, she needed to do this for her.

Richard had been right all along. She had been scared and frightened and weak. Her body may have been able to get up every time Winton had knocked it down, but her mind had hidden away somewhere she did not know. It had not gone far though, for she was able to retrieve it with alacrity when the time had come, but it had been hiding nonetheless. Her conscious thoughts had fled at the first sign of abnormality, of resistance, of the things that would make her different. Her husband had abused her, but as far as she knew, many husbands did the like, although she hoped not as severely or with such frequency as Winton had taken to it.

No, it was the other matter that had made her mind flee, her thoughts to go elsewhere, her conscience to resist acknowledging it.

She couldn't be a mother.

Her body did not seem to be equipped with all the proper and functioning parts. There was something *wrong* with her. That's what Winton had said. There was something innately wrong with her to not be able to produce an heir. It had not been noticed at first. It had all just been a game. The making of the new little earl. Only the game had gone on too long, and no one ever won. And then Winton beat her. She had honestly not expected it, and when it was all over, she forgave him for it. For she had carried the hurt in her as well. She knew what it felt like, knew the pain of it, knew the persistence of it. And yet, when Winton had reacted in the most objectionable way possible, she had *forgiven* him.

And it was this that had driven her to be sitting in front of a quasi-illegal gambling establishment for ladies on Piccadilly Street in London. This was what had driven her to the War Office six hours ago to make an oath she felt down to her bones. She was no longer going to forgive. She was no longer going to let her mind tell her she was unnatural and unworthy and deserving of something less. She was Lady Jane Haven, and she was about to thrash a woman at Pharo for the good of her country.

No apology necessary.

"Richard," she prompted when he did not move.

He looked at her, his face grim, and she leaned forward, pressing her lips to his.

"Richard," she said again, but this time her tone was thoughtful and coaxing.

Richard moved away from the door, tucking himself into the shadows at the opposite end of the coach.

"I'll be right here," he said.

She nodded, her hand brushing over his knee as she opened the door of the coach. The tiger jumped down immediately, helping her to step down in front of the Piccadilly house. The carriage door shut with a snap behind her.

"Good luck, my lady," said a voice behind her, and she looked up to the seat to see Daniels peering down at her. His eyes glittered in the lamplight, and standing there on the street in front of a known gambling establishment in the dark of a November night, staring up at a man who had helped her through more than one clandestine operation, Jane suddenly felt everything right itself. She drew a breath, shot Daniels a smile, and approached the house.

The door opened before she got to the last step of the stoop, and a butler dressed in silk brocade and fine leather gold-buckled shoes stood just inside the foyer.

"Lady Haven," he said with a bow, and Jane knew enough to not be surprised that the butler had called her by name, or at least not show it if she were. "Welcome," he said when he straightened, gesturing for her to enter.

She did so naturally, impressing even herself with her casual movements. As soon as she stepped inside the house, the smell of tobacco smoke hit her, followed shortly by the tinkling laughter of too many ladies in too small a space. The room was lavishly decorated. Too lavish by Jane's standards, but as it was a gentleman who had mustered the courage to operate such an establishment, she let it slip. As the butler took her wrap, a footman appeared, extending a tray of champagne, which Jane automatically helped herself to but did not partake. It would look odd if she did not imbibe, but she was here with a duty to accomplish. She needed a clear head, and although her heart remained unusually steady, she knew the alcohol would be unwise.

The butler escorted her into one of the drawing rooms found off of the main floor corridor. The room was bursting with ladies garbed in the most outrageous costumes Jane had ever witnessed. She laid a hand to her own skirts in a sudden feeling of discomfort. She had clearly underdressed for the occasion. A night at Fitzsimmons apparently not only included improper card playing but also an excuse to rediscover one's gaudiest ensemble.

The butler bowed to her before leaving and upon straightening, casually slipped a hand over her elbow. The touch was so brief she thought she had imagined it, but surely, such a touch was strictly forbidden by society's standards. She looked at the butler to find him watching her.

"The name is Hobbs, my lady, should you need anything."

The last word carried with it a weight of unspeakable proportions, and Jane suddenly realized why the butler knew her name. He was an agent with the Office.

She nodded in understanding and said, "Indeed," before turning away.

Jane immediately encountered several acquaintances who she was not surprised to find frequenting such an establishment. It was not as if Fitzsimmons was considered taboo. It was simply a rather daring endeavor for any woman to undertake. But nonetheless, society's ladies appeared to flock to the place for a bit of respite from everyday boredom. Jane knew she certainly would if it were not for the lectures at College.

She made her way from the front rooms that contained innocuous games of whist toward the back of the house. As she passed from room to room, the stakes raised precipitously until she reached the farthest drawing room, where all out gambling seemed to be taking place. This room was not as well attended as the front ones, and there was room to move from table to table. The space appeared to have been a small ballroom at one time, but it did not seem to have been used for such purposes for quite some time. Beneath her feet, the marble floors were scuffed with use, and the gilded framework about the doorways was dull with age. The entire grandeur of the room, although fine, was somehow muted, and it left Jane feeling a need for fresh air.

It was obvious that the occupants of the room did not feel in the least as Jane did. These were serious card players in here, focused intently on the cards in their hands or in the roll of the dice. Jane circulated the room until she spotted Lady Straughton standing beside a Pharo table as if waiting for a chance at play. Jane also recognized the banker at the table, one Mr. Grayson Mathers, a reliable agent at the War Office, that she had had the pleasure of meeting just that afternoon.

She placed her untouched champagne on the tray of a passing footman and approached the opposite side of the table at which Lady Straughton perched. Jane did not speak or in any way attempt to get Lady Straughton's attention. She let the game play on and quietly observed as did Straughton. It wasn't until the deck ended, and the ladies playing stood to open the table to other players, that Lady Straughton saw her.

The other woman instantly put a hand to her throat, her red satin gloves a startling contrast to her pale skin.

"Good evening, Lady Straughton," Jane said as she took one of the seats at the table.

She did not bother with preamble as it was clear that the matters between them were perfectly obvious. Lady Straughton had hired a man to kill Jane, and the man had not succeeded. Jane settled into her seat and waited to see if Lady Straughton would take the bait. If Straughton was any kind of player that Jane had heard her rumored to be, there was not a chance that she could resist such a temptation.

There was also not a chance that the woman would risk exposure by creating a scene.

It was true that the room was filled with ladies of a certain age that would no longer have a care for anything other than the planning of the week's dinner menus, but Straughton could not be too careful, regardless of her poor choice in leisure activities.

Straughton took the seat next to her, fanning out her skirts in careful arrangement. "Lady Haven, what a pleasant surprise."

Her voice carried the practiced lilt of a well-born French woman. She also smelled like toilet water, an indication that the woman used scents to cover up her smell from lack of bathing. Jane moved slightly away from the woman, adjusting her skirts so they did not touch hers. She placed her hands in her lap as she waited for the game to start. There was no reason to engage Lady Straughton in idle chatter. There was only the need to beat her at Pharo.

Technically, it would be the banker who would be winning or losing in this game, but if Jane could apply enough pressure by winning more than Lady Straughton, she believed the pressure would be enough to get the woman to break and confess her crimes. Jane just had to hope luck was on her side that evening.

"Good evening, ladies." Mathers bowed to both of them. "Are you both familiar with the rules of Pharo?"

Straughton was quick to nod, and Jane noticed the way her hands shook as she laid them on the edge of the table. The movement was imprecise, but Jane heard the way the satin of her gloves skittered over the green baize of the table.

Jane took this as a good sign that her presence was stirring the pressure she needed to secure the confession.

Jane placed a sum of money on the table, and Mathers quietly exchanged it for checks. Lady Straughton repeated the gesture but with noticeably less grace. Jane glanced slightly at the other woman, surprised to find her already flustered. It was not possible that this would turn out to be easier than she had believed, was it?

Mathers shuffled the deck of cards and placed it in front of Jane to split the deck. She did so, and Mathers returned the cards to his side to begin the game. The casekeeper had been reset from the previous game, and Jane looked at it, making note of each marker as if it determined precisely how long she had to see this scheme off. Each marker represented a card to be played in the game, a card that she could bet on turning up in the player's pile. If her card did in fact end up in that pile, she would win. If it ended up in the banker's pile, Mathers would. Jane only had to hope her card ended up in the correct pile.

"Place your bets, ladies."

Lady Straughton hastily placed a check on the seven card enameled into the green baize in the layout. Jane carefully set a check on the four. Mathers burned the first card from the pile and dealt the next two. The bets remained unsettled as neither card was drawn. Mathers continued to deal. The cards came fast, and the bets moved quickly. Jane watched as the markers on the casekeeper representing the cards played moved, each ticking off another chance for Jane to push Lady Straughton to the edge. She watched Straughton's movements carefully. Her gestures became more abrupt and hasty with each play, and with each play, Jane gained more confidence, for Jane continued to win.

She wondered briefly if Richard had somehow rigged the deck, but she had seen Mathers shuffle it as she had sat at the table. Straughton had seen it, too, for that matter. But no matter how Jane placed her bet, her card always seemed to come up in the winning pile. Just as Straughton's always seemed to appear in the banker's pile. Jane studied the case-keeper, noting which cards were left and placed her bets carefully. The deck was quickly disappearing, and when Straughton placed her bet on a card that had been exhausted, Jane knew she had the woman exactly where she wished her to be.

"It wasn't very nice what you did," Jane said, collecting her winnings from Mathers.

Straughton dropped a check on the layout. The piece skittered to Mathers' side of the table, and he carefully returned it to Straughton.

"I do not know what you mean," the woman said, her voice rushed, the syllables crashing into each other.

Mathers dealt, and Jane collected another win. Straughton's hands shook now as she placed a check on another exhausted card. There were four markers left on the casekeeper, and Straughton had not placed her bet on any card that could win. Jane smiled.

"*Je pense que vous faites,*" Jane said, and Straughton knocked her meager pile of checks from the table.

The woman stood so abruptly her chair fell over back-ward, knocking into a footman carrying a tray of champagne that fell in a waterfall of sparkling spirits. The commotion barely caused a ripple in the room as seasoned players focused on the game at hand. For a brief moment, Jane feared she had gone too far. She had wanted to upset Lady Straughton, unnerve her, even put her on edge, but she did not want to make the woman so manic that she lost coherent thought. If Lady Straughton did not retain some control, a confession was unlikely.

But then Lady Straughton swept her checks from the

floor where they had fallen and snatched up her overturned chair, taking a seat before a footman could so much as offer assistance. Jane did not dare look at Mathers then. For the first time, she felt her heart rate pick up, felt the palms of her hands grow damp in her gloves. She almost had her prey.

"I do not know what you speak of, but I think you speak of lies, Lady Haven," Lady Straughton whispered, her voice vacillating as her anger simmered.

"Lies?" Jane said. "I do not think I could tell a lie when it comes to someone taking my life."

Lady Straughton looked at her then. "Perhaps you should not be listening where you are not welcomed," she said, her voice suddenly heavy with her French accent.

Jane raised an eyebrow. "Do you mean in drawing rooms or in cemeteries?"

Jane watched as Lady Straughton's eyes grew wide, and her mouth formed a perfect *Oh* of astonishment. Jane smiled and returned to the game.

There were only four cards left. Mathers quickly dealt the next hand, and Straughton actually won. There wasn't a chance that the woman could catch up to Jane, but she knew that the last play held a certain amount of pride for Straughton. Now that Jane had made her aware of exactly where they stood, Straughton must feel the absolute need to win the next play.

Jane studied the casekeeper. There was an ace of hearts and a queen of diamonds left. She waited until Straughton quickly placed a check on the ace enameled on the baize. Jane placed her last check next to Straughton's on the ace, but before Mathers could deal, she also set a copper on top of the chip. Straughton let out a strangled gasp as Jane brought back her hand from the table. By placing the copper on the card, she was essentially calling Straughton an idiot, for Jane expected to see the ace show up in the banker's pile and not the players' pile. Nothing could have been more of an affront than the placement of that copper, and Straughton knew it.

Mathers dealt, and the ace of hearts fell onto the banker's pile.

Lady Straughton did not move at first. The woman was perfectly still as Mathers collected the bets and gave Jane her winnings. Jane felt her heart beat suddenly slow, and she drew in a deep breath, looking at nothing but the pile of checks in front of her.

And then Lady Straughton stood, leaning in so that her face was mere inches from Jane's. Jane saw the way the other woman's nostrils flared, and her pupils dilated.

"When the time comes for the revolution, you will be sorry you were so nosy," Lady Straughton hissed.

Jane raised a questioning eyebrow.

"The revolution that those bodies I snatched will pay for!"

Although a whisper, her statement was given with such force Jane knew Mathers had heard it as well.

Jane smiled. "You'll have to tell me how that revolution goes for you. It seems to be working out so well for the French."

Lady Straughton recoiled as if Jane had hit her.

"Make note, Lady Haven, my revolution will succeed. For me and my countrymen!" Now Lady Straughton was near to shouting, but the room was already abuzz with the conversations from the other game tables, and Jane doubted anyone had heard the woman.

"And which country would that be?" Jane asked, but Lady Straughton appeared to be finished with her.

She turned and left the room, but before she could make it into the corridor, Hobbs stepped through the door and latched a hand onto the woman's shoulder. "Lady Straughton, I will need you to accompany me. It seems you have an appointment with the authorities."

Jane let out a breath she hadn't realized she'd been holding and beckoned to the nearest footman. When he approached, she took a glass of champagne from his tray and drank the entire thing in one gulp.

* * *

RICHARD PULLED her closer against his body, cradling her in his arms. They lay there, spooned together on his bed, the bedclothes scattered about them as they had gotten into bed only to get as close to the other as possible. The bedclothes had become an unintentional casualty.

And in that moment, he swelled with pride, absolute pride that Jane was his. When he had heard what she'd done with the last bet, heard how she had undone Lady Straughton, he could do nothing but smile. The move was so classically Jane, he could not even be surprised by her actions. But he could be proud.

And now, although Richard held Jane as if she were a precious, fragile object, he knew now that Jane wouldn't break. Jane could not be broken. He had seen her physically damaged, emotionally crushed, and mentally tested, and nothing had even seemed to graze her delicate skin. Nothing. She was still Jane. She still smelled of lavender and lilacs and vanilla. She still smiled, her mouth wide and her cheeks full. She still laughed with the boys, the sound an undefinable pleasure.

She was still Jane after all of that, and she would still be Jane no matter what. But although he knew it, he also knew that it would take him time to adjust to it. He had only let himself see the battered and hurt Jane, a Jane that needed his protection. He had never let himself see the one who could protect him.

He knew he would slip up. He knew there would be times

when he made mistakes, when he thought her incapable of something he should not. And even as he knew it, he felt that Jane would forgive him, would teach him, would change his mind until he no longer made those mistakes. And he knew there would be time to let him.

"Marry me," he said then, feeling the words more deeply than he ever had before. "Marry me, Jane."

She stirred against him, turning her head to look at him, her eyes flashing in the firelight. Richard saw the bone aching tiredness there, saw the will to stay awake, to stay there in his arms. She smiled softly, and he saw in that smile satisfaction. She had not only secured a confession from a traitor, she had done so in close enough proximity to another agent so her story could be collaborated. Jane's first mission as a spy had been a resounding success, and he returned her smile there in the near darkness of his bedchamber. But then Jane's smile turned into something else. Something far more…dangerous.

"Is that the best you can do, Your Grace?"

Richard raised an eyebrow. "I beg your pardon, my lady?"

He had felt a niggling of fear when with the second time he proposed, she had still not given him a definitive yes, but there was something about Jane right then that was just the slightest bit mischievous. She nestled against him, bringing her hands up to stroke the hair on his chest. He found the touch distracting and swatted at her hands to keep her on task.

"Well, it's like this, Richard. My first marriage was arranged between my father and some old, stodgy patriarch I never met. And here I am on the verge of my second marriage, and all I get is a weak *marry me?*" She paused here to lick her lips, the gesture completely unnecessary, and he knew she was doing it to distract him. "It seems I require…more."

"More?" he heard himself say, but the voice seemed unusually far away.

Her hands moved down his chest now, lower and lower, until he snatched at one of them.

"More," was all that she said with the tiniest of shrugs.

She pulled her hand free and resumed its trail down his stomach and across his hip.

"More, my lady?" he said and pounced.

* * *

JANE COULD NOT DECIDE what was more unusual. The fact that, for the second morning in a row, she was having breakfast at the Lofton House without a care in the world for her reputation, or that just the night before she had been an integral part in the capture of a notorious traitor. That last bit may have been a touch exaggerated, but she was sure to be forgiven. Green spies were likely to get intoxicated on the rush of their first successful mission.

Jane felt a sigh come upon her as she descended to the main floor on her way to the morning room. If she were thinking of it as her first successful mission, it meant she was also thinking of more successful missions to come. And not once did the thought cause her panic or concern. Lady Jane Haven was indeed a spy for the War Office, and that was just a simple fact of circumstances. There was nothing odd or complicated about it. It was as if she had been a spy all along. She just hadn't signed on to the proper authorities yet.

She rounded the corner and came into the morning room to find it completely empty. Richard had left the bedchamber nearly an hour earlier to see to the boys, and she looked about the room as if he were hiding in it somewhere. She put her hands on her hips and looked up to the ceiling as if she could see what Richard and the boys were up to, but as she obviously could see nothing but the plaster ceiling, she shook her head and moved to her place at the table.

And stopped, her hands slipping from her hips.

Neatly arranged at her place setting was a piece of parchment, folded in half and set atop her plate like a tent. She picked it up carefully, taking in the details of the painting on the front of the paper. It seemed to be watercolors, a child's watercolors in particular. In clumsy strokes of paint were a man, a woman, and two boys, one smaller than the other. And next to the smallest boy, there appeared to be a dog. Jane raised an eyebrow at that part, but unfolded the parchment to see what was inside. There was a simple message. One she had heard twice before in a slightly different manner. The words *Marry us* were scrawled in a penmanship that looked strikingly like Nathan's handwriting, and below these words, three signatures in three different scripts were written.

Richard, Nathan, and Alec.

The tears came to her eyes and burned the back of her throat before she could draw another breath. She refolded the parchment on the words, but it did nothing to help her regain her composure. She reopened the parchment, taking in the simple message once more.

"Well, what's your answer?"

Jane spun around at the sound of Alec's small voice to find the three of them standing in the doorway, Richard with his two sons, each smiling more broadly than the next. Except Richard looked absolutely scared to death. And Jane's tears turned into a burst of laughter.

"Yes," she said. "Yes is my answer."

She crossed the room to Richard, wrapping her arms about him, feeling his arms close around her, stronger than they ever had before. She released him only long enough to pull the boys into her arms, squeezing them just as tightly. When she straightened again, she was pleased to see Richard no longer looked so terrified. Jane smiled and took one of his hands in hers before she remembered something. Holding up the parchment, she turned to the boys. "Is this a dog?" she said, indicating the creature next to the smallest boy.

Alec grinned. "It's a goat," he said. "I had Nathan add him."

Richard stilled beside her. "A goat?" he said.

Alec nodded, his grin growing bigger with every moment. "A brown goat. We should get one of those."

Nathan stood beside his brother, nodding affirmatively. "I agree. We should definitely get a goat," Nathan said.

Richard looked at her, his expression confused and lost. But then something moved over him, and a smile returned to his face. He looked back at the boys. "You must ask your mother," he said.

Jane gasped before she could stop it, swinging her gaze to his as he fought back the laughter.

"Richard Black, if you think you can start—"

"Mother, can we get a goat?" Alec interrupted, and everything in Jane stilled.

She looked at the small boy who had just called her the very thing she had thought she would never be, but that same little boy was already shaking his head.

"I don't think I want to call you *mother*. You're much more fun than the mothers I've met," he said, his tone deeply serious, and Jane couldn't help but laugh.

She knelt, taking Alec's hands into her own. "Alec, you may call me whatever you wish. And of course, you can have a goat. But you'll have to think of a name for it."

She squeezed his hands and stood, but Alec was already hopping impatiently on his feet.

"Oh, but I have. We'll call him Biscuit," he said.

Jane looked down at the smiling boy as his older brother tried to convince him that Biscuit was a terrible name for a goat. And then she turned to Richard, looking up at the man she would marry, free of doubts and concerns and fears. She loved this man, and nothing would ever change that.

"It appears your new wife comes with a goat," she said, stepping closer as his arms came around her once more.

"I wouldn't have it any other way," he said and kissed her.

ABOUT THE AUTHOR

Jessie decided to be a writer because the job of Indiana Jones was already filled.

Taking her history degree dangerously, Jessie tells the stories of courageous heroines, the men who dared to love them, and the world that tried to defeat them.

Jessie makes her home in the great state of New Hampshire where she lives with her husband and two very opinionated Basset hounds. For more, visit her website at jessieclever.com.

Printed in Great Britain
by Amazon